THE
Lost
ROYALS
SAGA

FATE OF THE FALLEN

RACHEL JONAS

CONTENTS

RACHEL JONAS

& NIKKI THORNE

DESCRIPTION

They've laid it all on the line—their lives, their love—
and now they can only hope it's been enough.

An unexpected turn of events has changed everything. Suddenly aware of a life more valuable than their own, Evie and Liam need a fail-proof plan to survive what's to come.

Only, with their enemies closing in ... they're out of time.

Their worst nightmares have arrived in full force and it will be impossible to avoid them all. So, when things fall apart, who will be the first to rise against them? Who will be the first to head into danger for the ones they love?

And worst of all ... which member of the Seaton Falls clan will lose everything?

As the story concludes, the stakes have been raised and no one is guaranteed to make it out unscathed.

Join Evie, Liam, and Nick in the fifth and final installment of THE LOST ROYALS SAGA.

Thank you for your purchase! I would love to get your feedback once you've finished the book!

Please leave a review and let others know what you thought of
"Fate of the Fallen"

Come hang out in the newly created "Shifter Lounge" on Facebook! https://www.facebook.com/groups/141633853243521/

We chat, recommend YA paranormal romances, and engage in other random acts of nerdiness. Once we're fully up and running, there will be tons of giveaways, exclusive ARC offers from me, and guest appearances by some of your favorite YA authors!

For all inquiries, please contact me using my primary email address:
author.racheljonas@gmail.com

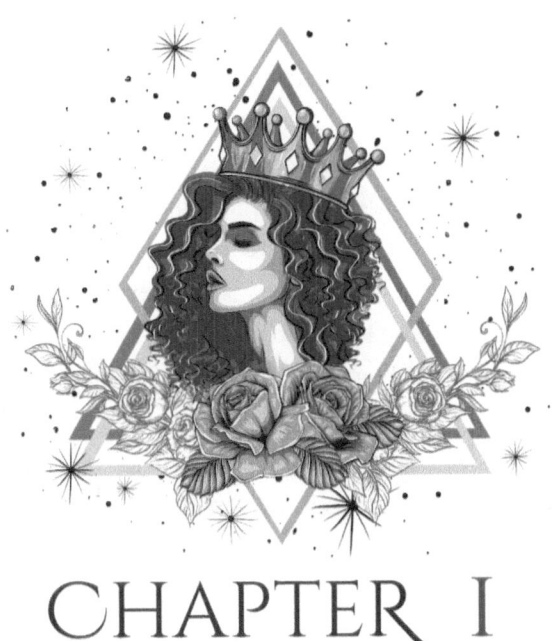

CHAPTER I

Nick

A blur of lights.

Disembodied voices.

A cacophony of both muted and hollow noises coming from every direction.

To top it all off, a putrid smell that brought me dangerously close to vomiting.

I felt and heard everything as I lie on the ground, my eyes fixed on a stone ceiling while I came to. I wasn't sure when I blacked out or how long I'd been in this state, which only added to the confusion. With the pain, the distraction of every sense being overloaded, I was only half sure of my location—a cell.

Again.

But unlike the other times, I was actually *grateful* this had been my fate, because it could have been much, much worse.

Should have been much worse.

Horrid images stuck with me although there was now a fair amount of distance between me and my mark—Evie. The desire hadn't left me despite no longer being in a blind rage. In fact, nothing would have pleased me more than to end her life. I had full knowledge of who she was, of what she meant to me then *and* now, and yet ... I could practically *taste* her blood in my mouth, feel her warm heart going still in the palm of my hand.

Hers, the other that beat twice as fast from deep within.

Suddenly sober, I turned onto my side, facing a wall marked with deep gashes, all in sets of five—claw marks from the many who'd occupied this space before me. I was thinking rationally now as the fog of a powerful spell lifted. A spell that, even in the overwhelming fit of rage, managed to hold me back. It proved that Evie's aunt was certainly a formidable force.

However, not even a witch as powerful as her could divert my path longer than a few minutes—hence the reason she insisted my brothers bring me here. She knew it was only a matter of time, too.

The fog clouding my memory was beginning to fade. I recalled feeling her magic slip bit by bit with each question she posed. The very fabric of it weakened, thinned as she forced me into submission. The awareness of the spell not being enough was only a reminder of one fact; there was no one, and nothing, strong enough to stop me.

Not for good.

Those deep markings in the wall were all there was to focus on, tangible evidence that this new realm I'd been made aware of wasn't so black and white. There were gray areas. Slivers of uncertainty where pariahs like myself could slip through the cracks and threaten the safety of our clans, of our species as a whole.

That was me; a blight on the supernatural world, an outsider.

My emotions were impossible to control—anger, fear, frustration and so much more. My head throbbed as each bombarded me, and among those thoughts was a realization; there were two heart-beats. Evie's, a child's.

There should have been comfort in finally having a major question answered, one that's haunted me since the beginning. I now knew what it meant to be triggered, knew what caused it, understood why my grandfather didn't stop himself the night he came for Evie.

He *couldn't.*

Not even my concern for her as a friend gave me pause. For him, with no emotional ties to her whatsoever, he didn't have a fighting chance.

This need to kill her, it was like a life source all its own, possibly the cause of the blackness that pulsed visibly through my veins. Suppressing a growl building in my chest, I made my way onto all fours, focusing on the sight of my knuckles pressed to the ground as I tried to stand. It was as though my limbs, my entire body, fought against me. Every part of me wanted nothing but to seek her out, finish what my grandfather started centuries ago. As ashamed as I was of these dark thoughts, it wasn't enough to make me want her dead any less.

My back fell against the cinderblock wall and I breathed deep. There was no way to know how long I'd be here, if I'd ever be allowed to leave.

No way of knowing if one day they'd rather I be dead than alive.

All thought left again when another wave of that putrid smell wafted in, so strong this time, I nearly doubled over with disgust. My first thought was that someone had expired in a nearby unit and the guards hadn't cared enough to dispose of the body. It wasn't like those locked down here were the Council's priority. It was quite possible I'd have to learn to live with the solitude, the uncertainty.

...And that godawful smell.

A nearby cot became a seat when I plopped down on the small thing, barely denting the stiff mattress placed on top. These were the arrangements, the accommodations deemed fitting for a criminal. A long breath passed between my lips as I acknowledged that's exactly what I was. A criminal.

To the Elders.

To the clan.

And now, to myself.

It felt like I'd done more wrong than right these days. No matter how hard I tried. Today—losing control, being unable to gain it back—was yet another shining example of that. I was officially a lost cause. For all I knew, I may have *always* been a lost cause.

My thoughts were interrupted, by a sound, one that chilled me to the bone despite it being a laugh. At first, I believed it to be that of a male, but then slightly higher pitched undertones made me think otherwise. Whatever the case ... it was the most uncomfortable, menacing sound I'd ever heard.

With both hands braced on the mattress, I stood, deciding to step closer with hopes that I'd get a look at whoever or whatever could emit such a noise. Gripping iron bars in my fists, I tried peering past them despite knowing it was impossible. The entire cell had been spelled, I'd sensed it the moment I came to. It was likely the work of many clan witches, because the power of one wouldn't have been enough to hold me.

The sound filtered in again and this time I was sure it was female, although still only vaguely distinguishable.

"Tell me ... are they having fun out there yet?" she asked, a hiss beneath every word spoken. "Because I've got a feeling the wait is finally over. The smell of war truly does excite my senses."

Another of those sinister laughs followed and I had no idea if she was even talking to me.

"Ah, yes," she crooned, her tone hinting at nostalgia with its deep rasp. "It's been far too long since we've had ourselves a good teeth-gnashing, soul-crushing war."

I stepped away from the bars when I accepted that I wouldn't get a glimpse of her, deciding instead to rest on the cot again.

"If you ask me, the earth seems ... *unsettled*. It's been far too long since it's had a taste of innocent blood seeping into its soil. After all," she went on, "we are but an extension of our exquisite planet. Therefore, at her core, she must be just as we are ... *unmistakably wicked*," she added with another laugh.

To say that I was uncomfortable would have been like saying the sun is *kinda* bright. Whoever this chick was, she weirded me out beyond belief. Especially with what she said next.

"It's okay to admit what you really are ... Nicholas," she uttered.

It honestly wasn't until my name was spoken that I was certain this conversation had even been meant for my ears. My senses were suddenly heightened as I blinked in the general direction of the bars that held me here. I wondered if she'd heard one of the guards mention who I was when I was brought down or ... if it was something else.

A short distance away, I listened as heavy fabric dragged across the aged stone, accompanying slow footsteps. The roughness of her palms could be heard even from here as they grazed and gripped a set of bars likely identical to mine. And this time, when she spoke to me, it was in a whisper that could not only be heard ... but felt.

All over.

Creeping across my skin.

"I know who you are," she taunted. "Or should I say ... I know *what* you are?"

The hairs on my arms and the back of my neck stood on end. A heavy drumming in my chest told of the way my heartrate spiked.

"I created you," she added. "Your very existence is all thanks to me. And even if others see you as nothing more than a curse, a scourge on your kind, I couldn't be prouder of what you've become. Without question, you are my most excellent creation."

Warm breath puffed from my nostrils and I nearly choked out a question, but knew better than to engage as the pieces began to fit. The way she tried to get inside my head with her words, that smell.

I'd encountered enough witches to know I was in the presence of one now. And judging by the odor, her soul had to be among the darkest that ever lived. Witches carried their essence with them in the form of an unshakable stench only detectable to other super-natural beings. The only I ever encountered without the trait had been Hilda.

"It's a pleasure to finally meet you," the wicked one went on, and there was no missing that she did, in fact, take pleasure in this opportunity. However, I took advantage of the fact that these walls and bars were spelled quite heavily and decided not to answer. She couldn't harm me, control me. She could only speak.

And *that* I could ignore.

It seemed to be a witch's nature to use trickery to ensnare others, like I'd allowed three to do in the not-so-distant past. That experience—and what it cost me and those I care about—taught me how quickly and easily these creatures could manipulate. So, I stayed silent, giving her nothing to use against me.

An amused sigh puffed from her lips before speaking again. "It's fine if you choose not to reply. We'll have our chance to meet soon enough," she promised.

I heard those rough, sandpaper-like hands of hers graze the bars again as her steps seemed to retreat. I pictured her—some vile, unimaginable creature—sinking into the darkest corner of her cell. For a moment, the space was completely silent. Eerily so, considering there were at least two of us locked away down here in the nothing.

Her cryptic statement spurred several thoughts. It was hard to tell if she actually knew something I didn't, or if this was a desperate attempt to bait me by planting doubt. Either way, I chose to trust my gut and didn't say a word.

I eventually stretched out on the cot, dangling one foot over the edge where it's length stopped accommodating mine, planting the other on the ground. Minutes turned into hours. So many I assumed it had to have been night by now. Although, with no windows to confirm, it was only a guess.

My lids got heavy from pure exhaustion, but I was far from comfortable. Every time I closed my eyes, images of impaled bodies decorating my grandfather's estate like macabre ornaments was all I saw. The sound of two sets of leather soles on the stone floor brought life back to my limbs. I got to my feet quickly and moved toward the bars, doing all I could to wait patiently for a glimpse of who ventured this deep into the Elders' chamber. However, as badly as I wanted out, I knew that wasn't likely to happen. Not so soon.

Maybe not ever.

At the sight of Richie's face—even riddled with distress and concern—I was happy to see him. After giving a tight smile that never reached his eyes, he nodded toward the guard who escorted him down. The two exchanged a knowing glance, and then it was just the two of us, my brother and I.

Of course, there was also the witch I was sure sat listening in a nearby cell.

"How bad is it?" I asked, still clutching the bars, finding the courage to ask more. "Am I a dead man?"

Richie's gaze lowered to the floor and it wasn't lost on me that he didn't rush to reassure me. Didn't rush to comfort me as my thoughts took a shift toward darkness. In other words, killing me was not off the table.

"We're doing everything we can," was his answer. A nondescript, open-ended answer at that.

My head lowered.

At the sight of him shifting something from his shoulder to his hand, I looked up again.

"I brought you a few things," he explained

It was a backpack, one he attempted to pass me through the bars. My eyes darted around my cell for a place to hide it. Maybe sensing the sudden spike in paranoia, Richie shook his head.

"No, it's fine. The Elders said it was okay to bring some of your stuff. Two guards checked it and said we were all good."

The thrumming behind my ears settled a bit and I knelt to sort through the items.

A handheld video game I hadn't played since who-knows-when, tons of batteries, a blank notepad.

I smiled up at him. "No pen?"

Richie pushed a hand to the back of his neck. "There uh ... there *was* one, but the guards didn't think that was a great idea," he shared.

Here I was, nearly nineteen years old, and no one trusted me with an ink pen. Not that I blamed them for knowing exactly who I was and what I was capable of. Who's to say I wouldn't actually hurt someone if I got desperate enough to get out of this cell?

Even *I* didn't find it hard to imagine.

"I'll bring you some crayons or um ... markers or something tomorrow," he offered.

I stared, realizing he was completely serious. The sound of a loud, humorless laugh leaving my mouth clearly startled him. It bounced off the cold, hard surfaces that surrounded us, an eerie sound that contrasted the general feeling of despair clinging to these walls.

... Crayons.

I really screwed up big this time.

Quieting down again, I stared motionlessly at the few remaining items Richie brought—two magazines, a deck of cards, and a watch. This was it, and while I was grateful to have *something* ... I now wanted out of this place even more than before.

Both arms throbbed as my veins began darkening again. I closed my eyes and concentrated on the one thing I trusted to bring me solace.

Roz.

Just like that, the tension began to disperse. Only, I now had a nagging feeling in my chest. I needed to hear her voice.

"Can I use your phone?" I practically begged

The question made Richie's brow twitch when he answered.

"I um ... I'm not sure that's allowed." He spoke in a whisper, inching closer to the bars that separated us; the bars that separated me from freedom, from committing an act so disgusting I felt like a monster just at the thought of it.

"Besides," Richie went on. "I probably don't even have a signal down here."

While under normal circumstances that would have been true, I knew better. During our stay at the Damascus Facility, I'd heard several staff members make mention of how good reception was just a few floors up on authorized levels. If they had capabilities to get clear signals *that* deep, I knew it was possible here, too.

"Can you just ... check?" I asked hopefully, glancing at the pocket where a rectangular-shaped imprint had drawn my attention.

Several seconds passed, but then his fingers twitched a bit and I knew he was considering it. It wasn't until he sighed deeply and reached toward his hip that I knew he caved.

"Make it quick," he grumbled, glancing left and right before placing my one link to the outside world in my hand.

"Thank you," I said in a rush, darting toward the back of my cell, already dialing Roz's number.

It rang, and with each tone my stomach sank a little lower.

"Hello?"

The sound of her voice drew a deep breath from my lungs. Right away, I felt lighter, like a ginormous weight had been lifted off my shoulders. The darkness within even seemed to recede just a bit.

"Nick, is that you?" She was nearly frantic when asking, but kept her voice low. If I had to guess, word of my behavior had spread and her father wouldn't appreciate me calling.

"It is, and I'm okay, but ... I won't be able to see you for a bit and I didn't want you to worry," I sighed, vaguely explaining my circumstances.

"Too late," she replied, her voice clearly trembling when she went on. "I'm already worried. I can ...*feel* it," she explained.

I wasn't sure what that meant, so I asked, "Feel what?"

"That you're different," she blurted. The words came without thought because she didn't doubt them for a second. She *knew* I'd been triggered.

Because, like she said, she felt it.

I had no idea how that was possible, if it was normal or just an '*us*' thing, or just a *Roz* thing.

"After I left your place this morning, when I got back home, there were people here," she added, her words drawing my focus in completely.

"People?" I asked.

"Yeah. As in ... an Elder, the Chancellor," she added.

I frowned, immediately thinking this had something to do with me, with the bodies, or ... something, but when she said more, I knew that wasn't the case.

"Nick, I ... there's something you need to know," she began. "Something's happening to me. I told you some of it—like my dad not being able to control me like before—but ... apparently there's more to it than that," she scoffed, sounding confused and distant. I couldn't help but to wish I was there with her, in the flesh to comfort her through whatever this 'something' might have been.

"Are you ... okay?" I asked, unable to deny my concern.

"I can't really get into it right now, but I'll try to explain when I can," she promised, pivoting the conversation again the next second. "Is there anything I can do to help. Anything I can say to the Council?" she offered.

The question was sincere and the innocence of it brought out a smile I didn't even know I had in me.

"I wish, but ... no," I sighed. "I don't think there's anything *anyone* could say at this point."

The reality of that was all I could think about until Roz spoke again.

"Well, what changed?" she asked. "What made the switch get flipped? Was it the bodies?"

My eyelids drifted closed as I recaptured that moment, the instant the intent of my visit had gone from wanting to warn Evie, to wanting to feel her blood on my hands.

"Evie's ... she's ... there's a kid," I forced out, painfully aware of how hard those words were to say.

It was more than just feeling ashamed that my sinister intentions to kill became even more wicked knowing she carried a child. It was also strange to think of her in that way. Strange to think of what this all said of her deepening connection to Liam.

A familiar feeling pinged in the center of my chest and I forced it into submission with the acknowledgement of what it was —a stray trace of emotion that had no place in my life for so many reasons.

Jealousy.

Roz had grown to mean something to me, more than what I ever saw coming. Plus, I'd long since accepted that Evie and I were only ever meant to be friends. Still, there was no denying the burn I felt at the thought of how this all came to be.

Her.

Together with him.

Close in ways I always tried to convince myself she wouldn't even consider. However, the proof was the second heartbeat. It made it impossible to ignore that they were intimate in every sense of the word.

At the sound of Roz's voice, I realized my fists were clenched into tight fists.

"What are the Elders saying?" she asked, that quaking in her voice still evident.

I shook my head as if she were here in the flesh, having this conversation face-to-face.

"They haven't said anything yet. At least not to me," I added, glancing up toward Richie as he paced.

"Isn't there a way we can—"

I cut her off, knowing the rest of that statement was about to infect us *both* with false hope.

"No, there's nothing," I said flatly. "And I have to end the call. I shouldn't even be doing this, I just ... I wanted you to know I was okay," I explained, adding more than I intended to share just a moment ago. "And I wanted ... I needed to hear your voice."

Roz was silent on the other end, maybe letting the full breadth of the situation sink in.

"Promise you'll send word whenever you can? *However* you can?" she added.

"Of course," I promised.

A lingering silence hinted that we both had more to say, but then the line went dead. Over the last few months, my feelings for Roz had deepened more than either of us saw coming. However, expressing those feelings hadn't been easy. And now, the idea of telling her under *these* circumstances—while I was locked in this cage, while she was dealing with her own stuff—would have been the worst possible timing yet.

"Everything good?" Richie asked when his phone was safe in his pocket.

I let go of a sharp breath before answering. "She's safe. That'll have to be enough for now."

I didn't mention what she said about an Elder and the Chancellor being at her house when she made it home this morning.

Richie nodded and I knew him well enough to recognize he was at a loss right now. He'd gotten so used to being in control and having all the answers, he didn't seem to know quite what to say in this moment—when my freedom, my *life*, hung in the balance.

"I'll uh ... I'll get back as soon as I can with updates," he blurted. "Me and some of the guys are heading out to take care of something in a bit."

I stared at his feet when he turned, not understanding what there was for him to take care of. However, I could only focus on the fact that he'd be on his way soon, leaving me down here to go insane in the silence.

His gaze lifted to meet mine when he spoke again. "I'm doing everything I can, Nick."

The promise was heartfelt, and I knew he meant it. For now, it was the only thing I could cling to.

I passed a dim, cynical smile his way when I nodded. "I know. Be here when you get back."

CHAPTER 2

Liam

T he number of guards outside had tripled since morning, and rightfully so considering how our circumstances changed. This—the sitting, the waiting—was unnerving. It wasn't in my nature to sit idle, but rather to take action in times like these. And now, with the arrival of nightfall, it was time to do just that.

The first step toward retaliation was a recon mission. We had to see what we were up against. Sebastian had already made two bold statements—the flood, and then the bodies left to rot on the property of the Stokes estate. Meanwhile, we'd done nothing, but that would finally change once we knew what tricks he had up his sleeve. And as soon as we did, a hell storm would be unleashed on him, on his army.

I'd make sure of it.

We had it on good authority the Sovereign was holed up about thirty miles north in Ridge Borough—a now abandoned fishing town just off the shore of Lake Huron. There hadn't been residents to speak of in decades, so the landscape was mostly historical landmarks and dilapidated buildings; perfect for a band of murderers needing to hide out while plotting their next move in secret.

The guys and I were done being spectators as things went awry in Seaton Falls, done waiting for the Council to give the command to strike. They might disapprove of our insubordination, but so be it. Tonight, fewer than a dozen of us would take matters into our own hands, doing what we deemed necessary to protect those we love—with or *without* the Council's permission.

On several occasions, I heard Elise, Hilda and others mention that our war was soon to begin. This was clearly the opinion of those who had limited engagement in combat. They hadn't stared war in its cruel, dark eyes like I had. More often than not, it came quietly. Not in a storm of battle cries or courageous stampedes toward the enemy. The war Sebastian waged on us had been underway for quite some time already. Starting when he showed up in Seaton Falls with ill-intent, attempting to capture Evangeline, instead settling for me. Again, when he wreaked havoc on the residents by flooding the valley. War wasn't just about massive displays of firepower or hand-to-hand engagement. While I was sure it would one day come to a heated crescendo ... this fight had arrived at our door months ago.

The motive behind his latest tactic—dead bodies littered across the lawn—was unclear, but it was a threat nonetheless. Whether one to the entire clan or Nick personally, we couldn't let it go unchecked. Doing so would send a message of weakness, passivism. Sebastian made it known he'd only keep hitting us harder and closer to the heart each time.

This fact made tonight's mission one-hundred-percent necessary, and the guys all agreed—Elise's boys, Dallas, the Stokes brothers. Our hands were tied for a while, but now that our numbers had swelled, we stood a chance at turning things in our favor.

Finally.

The only thing that kept me sane while waiting for the signal to head out was lying here, holding Evangeline in the darkness. As if she knew the power being near her had over me, warmth spread through my chest when she nestled her head against it. The others had left us in peace for the better part of the day, although I knew that hadn't been an easy thing to do. Their concern for her ran almost as deep as mine.

Especially now that their concern was no longer just for her, but also ... for the child.

Our child.

The stark contrast of life and death surrounding us was difficult to fathom, starting with the information Nick had come to deliver. Seeing him triggered brought back memories that were always so alive inside my head they hardly felt like memories at all. They were more like nightmares I relived every day with my eyes wide open.

Every time Evangeline smiled.

When I held her.

I'd never forget seeing that beast flee with her clasped beneath his arm, stealing more from me than just a physical body.

She was my entire life.

My gaze lowered to her stomach with that thought, despite it being too early for her to show. Before today, we had no clue as to her condition, but ... she held something so precious within her, so fragile. I didn't think it was possible to feel more protective over her than I already did, but now I knew how flawed my thinking had been. Not only was I responsible for *her* life, I was also responsible for the one we created.

Together in love.

"I'm scared," she breathed, letting the words leave her lips in a rush.

"If you're talking about tonight, there's nothing to worry about," I assured her. "We're just following up on a lead Dallas was given."

She shook her head, letting me know I misunderstood. "No, not just that. It's ... I don't know what's supposed to happen from here. After today—with Nick, with Sebastian—everything's changed. And now ... a kid."

Evangeline pushed a hand through her dark curls, releasing another breath before adding, "I don't even know where to start, what moves are the right moves, what my priorities are supposed to be. It's just ... everything's happening so fast."

She was on the verge of spiraling. When water pooled in the corners of her eyes, I acted quickly to reel her back in. At the feel of my hand against her cheek, she peered up at me.

"You're mine. Whatever it takes to bring you through this, whatever it takes to keep you safe ... it's as good as done," I assured her, and I meant every word. Our growing family would *always* be my top priority.

Always.

She stared, those tears still threatening to fall, but I imagined for a very different reason now than before. She knew how fiercely she was loved. By me, by so many others.

Today, in the blink of an eye, our entire game plan had changed. I was never keen on the idea of having her fight at my side, but was comforted knowing she'd come into her own and was capable of doing so. However, now, I wanted nothing more than for her to be kept as far away from Sebastian and his army as possible. There were several reasons, but one in particular stood out above the rest.

He couldn't, under any circumstances, know she was with child.

And that could become a challenge much sooner than Evangeline may have realized.

Her being a hybrid complicated things. The experience of bringing a child into the world was drastically different for a lycan female than a dragon and her condition could manifest in either manner. In short, there was no way to predict the path her body would follow—that of a wolf or that of a dragon. Had this been months ago, I would have been sure, but since her lesser side had been so prevalent lately, it was unclear.

A lycan female's term was similar to that of a human, but with the additional discomfort of birthing larger offspring. For a dragon, the process was drastically different—abbreviated and more intense physically, emotionally, a fact that some argue may be proof our strength and ferocity starts in the womb. Trying to guess which turn this would take was impossible, but if Evangeline's dragon *did* decide to dominate her term, she'd be vulnerable a lot sooner than she was likely expecting.

We *all* would be.

Smooth skin met my fingertips where I stroked the side of her neck.

"How bad do you think things will get?" she asked. Her voice was quiet, as if she might be afraid to hear the answer.

Under normal circumstances, I would have shielded her. However, she made a request what seemed like a lifetime ago. She asked that I always tell her the truth, even the hard truths.

This was definitely one of those times.

"They'll uh ... they'll get bad, but we'll take it one day at a time, think through our options, strategizing the best plan of action before we strike," I explained.

It became apparent she didn't care for that term—*strike*. When she glanced up the next moment I was sure of it. Her pulse throbbed where my thumb rested against her throat. I hated being the one to do this, being the bearer of bad news. If for no other reason than to avoid the way she looked at me now, with fear and dread flooding in.

"Hilda will do all she can to hide you, starting the moment she gets back from speaking with the Elders," I promised. "She'll use heavier spells on the house, most likely." I paused before making another suggestion, one I was sure Evangeline would object to. "Or maybe ... it'd be best if we ... take you somewhere outside of town."

Silence, just like I expected, but this had been on my mind all day. Removing her from the equation, getting her as far away from here as possible, was our best option.

"No," she said flatly.

Of *course* she said no.

She glanced up and my eyes searched hers. "Evangeline ..."

"No," she repeated. Her response didn't change, nor did her resolve. "I'm not gonna run from this. Hilda can cast her spells or do whatever magic she wants, but I'm not leaving town," she clarified.

I breathed deep and the bed shifted a bit when she leaned away, sitting straight.

"The whole point of this has been that, when the dust settles, when this war is over, I'll stand in Sebastian's place, right? The lycans are supposed to revere me as their queen, aren't they?" she asked.

Refusing to answer, air rushed from my lungs as I stared at her. She didn't get it. I couldn't have cared less what everyone wanted from her, what their expectations were concerning who or what she would one day become. Keeping her alive ... that was the *only* thing I cared about.

"I can't expect them to trust me if we don't stand in solidarity, Liam. If I'm off on some glorified vacation while they're cut down in battle ... they'll never respect me."

She stared off, surprising me with how she'd come into her

own without even realizing it, reminding me of Elise in so many ways. She had heart, integrity. She was fair and believed in second chances. Sometimes third and fourth chances, too.

And let's not forget the inherited stubbornness.

There was no crown on her head just yet, but it was unmistakable that the girl I ran into in an alley so many months ago had evolved, had blossomed into a formidable woman.

A queen.

Still, no matter how honorable her intentions, I disagreed.

The dark eyes that had been my undoing since the beginning of time stared through me even now, as I was certain fear welled in her stomach just like it did mine. You wouldn't have known it, though. Before me, she was the picture of bravery and determination.

"I won't run from this, Liam," she asserted once more.

It killed me inside, knowing I couldn't *make* her bend to my will. She'd always had her own mind, her own way of doing things, and neither death nor rebirth had changed that.

Still, I had to make one final plea.

My palm settled against her stomach. It was still crazy to think we created a life, but soon there'd be no mistaking it.

When my fingers splayed across her warm flesh—the only thing separating me from our child—Evangeline's eyes flitted with doubt. It was slight and only lasted half a second, but it was there. I needed her to understand this wasn't just about her and I.

There was another whose existence, I believed, we both agreed mattered even more than our own.

"And what if things get out of hand?" I uttered, peering up again at the sound of the tremor in my own voice—the sound of a desperate man who couldn't stand the thought of losing his family.

"What if it turns bad too quickly and there's no time to get you to safety?" I added.

Our perspectives on this were so different, Evangeline's and mine.

A world apart I was sure. In my eyes, she was far beyond her years, and discovering what triggered Nick ... it meant we'd been in this position before. In another lifetime, life grew within her, life neither of us had a chance to become aware of, and I was doing everything I could to pretend that part didn't make all the difference, but ... it did.

Knowing I failed them *both* that night ... I couldn't let that happen again.

My eyes closed at the feel of her hand to my cheek, at the feel of the love that one touch conveyed.

"We just have to keep believing this hasn't all been for nothing, Liam—the pain, the fight ... the loss," she breathed.

Maybe she was stronger than me, capable of suspending reality longer than I was used to doing, because we clearly saw this ending two different ways.

"A keeper," I blurted, bringing confusion to her expression when I uttered the term.

"A ... what? What's a keeper?"

"It's an old phrase," I explained. "One that hasn't been used in our realm in centuries, but mostly because it hasn't applied. In short, it's a female warrior assigned to an expectant noblewoman. Her sole duty would be to watch over you. To tend to you and protect you at all cost."

Evangeline said nothing, so I wasn't sure how this was going over.

"I could send for someone," I added. "I have allies overseas. I've crossed paths with some of the fiercest female shifters walking the Earth. Right off the top of my head, I can think of three who—"

"Liam, stop."

My lips stayed parted when she cut me off midsentence and I stared. A soft breath passed between Evangeline's lips and I knew she was getting ready to kill this option just like she'd killed the others.

"I can't ... It isn't fair to ask someone to put their life on the line for me. To ask them to leave their families, their homes," she added, falling silent before finishing her thought.

It dawned on me that she might have been reflecting on her own life, how she'd lost so much. Being a woman of integrity, having such a big heart, she'd never dream of letting me ask someone to walk away from their loved ones to protect her.

I understood. I *hated* it, but ... I understood.

I was fully prepared to plead my case one last time, beg if I had to, but a knock at the door stole my chance. Unspoken words burned in my throat, needing to be said sooner rather than later. For a moment, I considered telling whoever interrupted to come back a little later, but a second, more urgent pounding finally got me off the bed.

I snatched the door open and my solemn expression was met by six impatient stares—Evangeline's brothers.

The bed creaked behind me, followed by the sound of soft feet padding across the floor. The feel of a warm hand pressed gently to my back the next second was expected. The guys' gazes shifted to Evangeline where she now stood beside me, leaning into my side despite our disagreement.

She greeted them with a smile that hid her true feelings, the fear and concern she was only willing to expose to me.

"Sorry to interrupt, but the others are here," Josiah said first. "One of the guards just informed Dallas that they're waiting at the gate."

A deep breath left my mouth. It was time to head out, but I didn't like the idea of leaving this conversation unfinished, didn't like the idea of leaving with such an important issue unresolved.

Evangeline turned to face me, a weary smile on her lips.

"Go," she urged softly. "We'll talk when you get back."

We both knew that wouldn't be until morning, but there

wasn't much choice. Before letting me out of her sight, she stretched up on the tips of her toes and kissed me once.

"Please, be careful," she said before glancing at each of her brothers when adding, "*All* of you."

They nodded, assuring her they'd try, and I did the same.

"Before we go," Josiah piped, "there was something we wanted to say earlier, but weren't sure the time was right." He paused, standing front and center as he held Evangeline's gaze. "We're aware the circumstances aren't ideal, but—"

"But it seems congratulations are in order," Ethan interjected, finishing his brother's thought with a huge grin.

Yeah, this brood was amped up to go spy on Sebastian's operation tonight, but this energy they exuded was something else. Excitement, brought on by the idea of there being a new addition joining our family in the coming months.

"The arrival of a child is always something to celebrate," Ivan added, speaking with the same air of decorum as the others, a sound that had long since faded from time.

I managed a smile. A genuine one as I uttered a response. "... Thank you."

My shoulder was shaken hard when Declan gripped it as he spoke. "Still as virile as ever. My guess? It will be a strong, healthy boy," he said with certainty.

In our time, every man wanted a son—one he could teach to be strong and fearless. However, life experience had taught me to be grateful with fewer conditions. Whether Evangeline carried my son or daughter, I simply wanted him or her to arrive in this world safely.

Tobias rolled his eyes with a laugh, maybe acknowledging how blatantly macho Declan's statement had been. "Girl or boy, we'll be overjoyed," he assured me.

Beside him, Declan shrugged before defending himself. "Of course we're happy just to add to the family," he quipped, but then leaned in with a grin to say more. "But Father always believed it was the work of a *real* man that made a boy," he laughed, slamming a heavy fist to my bicep with the joke.

Evangeline smiled, but I didn't miss the redness that spread across her cheeks.

Caleb reached for her hand, placing a kiss to the back of it. The adoration in his gaze was apparent when he all but bowed to her. "Forgive the crassness of the others," he smiled. "We're just excited."

Evangeline's smile broadened at his words.

"Thank you," she stated. "I ... honestly think I'm a little excited, too?" The comment left her mouth as more of a question than a fact. Her gaze was riddled with surprise when she turned to me. As if feeling this way was a shock to even *her*.

The confession made my heart sputter inside my chest, hearing that this news hadn't been all bad in her eyes. I wasn't sure that would be the case at first, especially because she's been under the illusion that what she remembers is all there's been to her life. But it was now clear I underestimated her growth, her maturing perspective.

Delicate fingers slipped between mine and I squeezed them, feeling the closeness we shared grow even deeper.

"We'll wait for you outside," Josiah concluded. "Dallas would like to talk strategy while we travel. He says the Council's holding a meeting tomorrow and we'd like to be prepared," he added.

"Sounds good," I nodded, feeling like I was being tugged in two different directions as they walked away. On the one hand, I knew the importance of getting out in front of whatever stunt Sebastian might try to pull next. On the other, I wanted to be here, wanted to finish the discussion.

I glanced down at Evangeline before bringing her close. "We'll finish sorting things out in the morning," I promised.

Her cheek tensed against my chest with what I guessed to be a smile. "Okay," she replied, "but I still won't change my mind."

Even if she hadn't said as much, I wouldn't have expected anything else.

I gripped her tight, bringing a laugh out of her that fueled my very soul. "We'll see about that. I can be pretty persuasive when I need to be."

She didn't miss the hidden meaning behind the words when I buried my face in her neck, kissing her one last time.

"Be safe and don't try to be a hero," she said with a smile.

It took a moment, but my hold on her eventually loosened and I tore myself away.

'If you need me … for anything," I clarified, *'don't hesitate.'*

Her smile grew at the sound of my thoughts echoing inside her head instead of speaking them aloud. Maybe because she missed that part of our connection as much as I had.

'You have my word,' she promised.

CHAPTER 3

Liam

"Fellas, I think it's time to consider we might have a traitor within the clan," Dallas breathed, staring straight ahead as Richie drove.

We were eleven deep, packed into the bed of a pickup nearing the outskirts of Seaton Falls. Until now, it'd been a quiet ride with several miles ahead of us before reaching Ridge Borough, but Dallas had just changed that. He opened the floor to discuss something I think we had all considered and simply hadn't said aloud. My reason being that I still wasn't sure who could be trusted, who might be the mole leaking information to the Sovereign.

Richie glanced over his shoulder from the cab, clearly interested in Dallas' theory. "Took the words right out of my mouth," he grumbled.

"It's the only thing that makes sense," Dallas went on, resting his elbows on his knees as the truck shook and swayed over uneven terrain.

"I thought it was just me," Ben chimed in.

Dallas shook his head and shared more. "Think about it. The likelihood of it being brought up in a Council meeting that the Elders were planning to use the excuse of a faulty dam to evacuate the town, and then within a couple days that very thing happens ... it's a pretty big freakin' coincidence," he concluded.

"Any thoughts on who it could be?" Tobias asked, glancing around to see who might answer.

"Only thing I know for sure is it isn't anyone in this vehicle," was the only answer Dallas had to offer. "Out of *everyone,* we've got the most at stake. Our families are all at the heart of this thing. So, as far as I'm concerned," he said, glancing around, "we need to make a pact, right here and now, to stick together."

"Agreed," several said in unison while others nodded to show they were on the same page.

"And whatever we discuss concerning strategy, should stay between us and the Elders," Kyle interjected.

I had something to add and all turned when I chimed in for the first time, lifting my gaze from the floor of the truck bed.

"Evangeline's condition ... that stays between us, too. Not even the Elders need to know as far as I'm concerned."

The expressions the group displayed reflected their compassion. I could only believe it meant that each understood why I, perhaps more than anyone, had so much riding on this newly formed alliance.

"You have our word on that."

The declaration had come from Richie and I didn't miss the conviction in his tone, the assurance that we were all fighting on the same team. It told of how he sympathized with my willingness to go the distance for my family. He recognized it because he'd do the same for his. Even if neither of us would admit it, we were a lot alike—both hellbent on protecting our loved ones.

At all costs.

It didn't matter that, traditionally speaking, dragons didn't form packs. Being raised in a kingdom where both species held equal rule, my perspective was different. As I rode in the truck, a dragon to my left, my hybrid brothers surrounding me, and a well-respected witch among our household, there was no denying our family was just that.

A pack.

"Way I see it, with Sebastian on his way out, Evangeline's *already* queen," Richie said in a calm, matter-of-fact tone as he watched the road. "I mean, what good are we if we can't protect her, you know?"

I smiled at that, at how he had already begun to hold Evangeline to the same high regard the Council had. As the representative alpha of his pack, it was important that he, in particular, stood with me.

"I appreciate that," I said. When I nodded his way, he did the same.

We hadn't always seen eye-to-eye, but had grown to respect one another. Trusting he'd do everything in his power to aid my efforts to keep Evangeline safe, that respect only deepened.

We were all silent for a moment and I thought over the implications of what it truly meant to have a mole in Seaton Falls. What had they heard? What information had they taken back to Sebastian? How would we ever figure out who wasn't truly on our side?

"We've all got your back."

I turned to Dallas when he nudged me. To my surprise, he was even smiling a bit. "It's not every day a man finds out he's gonna be a father. Just know, if our lives were normal, we'd be heading out to grab a few celebratory drinks tonight, not ... hunting down a madman."

"In my opinion," Caleb chimed in, "what we've set out to do tonight will be far more entertaining." He let out a hearty laugh and the others joined him, but my thoughts were on other things, hung up on one word Dallas said.

Father.

Of all the roles I'd filled, that was one I honestly never imagined I'd have a shot at. I let go of the idea when I lost Evangeline, and this time around, we hadn't had a moment's peace to even *think* about the future, so to say this had thrown me for a loop was an understatement.

... A father

It was so hard to wrap my head around that.

Noah had been nurturing and levelheaded when he raised us. I wasn't sure I could be either of those things. However, as I sat trying to picture it, a phantom squeeze to my finger had me imagining a small hand holding onto it. That feeling, imagining what it would be like to finally have it all ... it was enough to make me want to try. It made me determined to be everything to this kid Noah had been to me. It was enough to make me certain I'd never *stop* trying, even if I didn't always get it right.

This ... was happening.

The circumstances were scary for too many reasons to name, starting with Evangeline's refusal to leave, but now that I started, I couldn't stop myself from envisioning what our future might look like. Envisioning what the embodiment of a lifelong love story would look like.

As hard as I fought the notion, for fear of losing it all ... I wanted it, wanted everything that had already been stolen from me once before.

My family.

"I appreciate that," I eventually said, remembering to respond to Dallas as I emerged from deep thoughts.

I gave a half smile, one I guessed might be hard to read. These circumstances were twofold. It came with the realization that my role, my inherent duty to protect the one I love, was now twice as important.

Twice as difficult.

Dallas, being perceptive, seemed to sense I didn't want to talk about it, didn't want to go deeper into this conversation than we already had. Luckily, he changed the subject, turning his attention toward Ben and Kyle.

"Were you able to get the situation at your grandfather's place taken care of?" he asked.

At mention of the bodies, both their expressions dimmed.

"We uh ... we took care of it," Ben stammered. "Buried a good fifteen or twenty before deciding to burn the rest for the sake of time."

There was no missing the remorse that riddled his tone—sympathy for those who'd been cut down for the sole purpose of the Sovereign proving some vague point.

"Did anyone show up to help?" Dallas asked next, folding both arms across his chest. He hadn't said as much, but I knew he would've been there if he could have. However, with the new guards that showed up to secure the house, he'd been busy showing them the ropes a better part of the day.

Kyle gave a nod. "A few of the guys who usually work Nick's shift volunteered when they caught wind of what happened."

Just hearing Nick's name made my blood run hot, fire threatening to explode from my palms.

"How *is* your brother? Is he ... stable now?" Ivan asked, directing the question toward Ben.

It didn't surprise me to hear an air of sensitivity beneath the words, even after Elise explained to him and his brothers that Nick was the Liberator incarnate. Regardless of what Nick represented to *us*, he was still just a kid in the eyes of his family, and Ivan hadn't forgotten that.

A nod came first. "Seems to be doing better," Ben shared. "Richie stopped in to see him before we got started with ... *cleanup.*"

"He's still not himself, but definitely more in control than when he left here," Richie clarified from behind the wheel. "His emotions aren't quite in check yet, but we have hope that'll change with time."

I heard them, believed *they* believed these claims, but I didn't trust Nick any more now than I did when he was in a full rage outside the gate.

"Well, one thing's for sure," Dallas said, rearing back with a stretch as the truck bounced over a shallow pothole, "we're all rooting for him to fight this."

No one said a word, but the range of emotions was evident on every face. Caleb and Declan clearly didn't share Dallas' sentiment as a look passed between them. Meanwhile, Josiah, Tobias and Ethan were definitely sympathetic to the torment Nick's state was putting his brothers through. Ivan, like me, wasn't giving much away. However, if I had to guess, we were of the same mind. We'd sit back quietly for the time being, for the sake of alliances, but I believed he was also willing to go after Nick with all he had in him if it came down to that.

"Now that we're all on the same page," Dallas announced, "I suppose now is as good a time as any to figure out what we *do* know, so we can figure out what we *don't* know."

Ben agreed. "Well, for starters, I'm not totally convinced leaving all those bodies was a warning."

Intrigued, we all turned to face him. Even Declan shifted from his seat up front to pay attention.

"I'm not sure what he could possibly do with the info, but for what it's worth ... I have a hunch Sebastian knows exactly what Nick is," was Ben's next statement. "I think he knows and the bodies had something to do with that. I mean, why else would he choose him? It can't just be because he was there that day we went with Evie. We were *all* there," he reasoned. "I think he knows and it's not lost on him that something changes in Nick every time he kills."

Before now, none of us had acknowledged this as a fact, but I couldn't have agreed with Ben more.

"I've seen it with my own eyes," he added. "First with the mutts, again when we trekked to the U.P. Each time, he drifts a little deeper into the darkness. So, what better way to taunt the killer within him than to bring death, literally, right to his doorstep?"

A booming voice rang out from the front and my gaze shifted right to Richie when he scolded his brother.

"Choose a better word," he demanded, clarifying what he meant right away. "Don't ever refer to him as a killer."

Ben tensed and immediately jumped to defend himself. "I didn't say he was a killer," he reasoned. "I said *'the killer within him'*. I'm aware there's a difference."

The rest of us were silent, waiting for Richie's reaction. Even from where I sat I saw his jaw working, his grip tightening on the steering wheel when he spoke again.

"Choose ... a better ... word," he seethed, repeating himself.

Ben scoffed. Having been put in place by his brother clearly didn't sit well, but he had no choice but to obey his alpha.

"You're right," he conceded, clearly only saying more out of obligation. "Next time, I'll ... be more careful with what I say, I guess."

He went quiet after that, turning to watch the endless woods fly past as the miles between us and Seaton Falls climbed.

"Long story short," Kyle said, taking over the conversation, "we don't think Evie's in any more danger today than she was yester-day. If that message truly was just for Nick, with the increased security and sigils on your property, we believe she's safe," he concluded.

While I appreciated his take on things, I wouldn't buy into his ideas so easily.

Again, I imagined the relief I would've felt if Evangeline had just … given in. If she'd just taken pity on me and let me hide her away somewhere no one, including Sebastian, could find her.

But she wouldn't even consider it.

"So, this is another vote for there being a mole among us," Dallas chimed in, referencing Ben's theory. "If someone told them about our plan for the falls, that same someone could have let the cat out of the bag about Nick."

The others nodded in agreement.

"Are we positive our intel for tonight's mission wasn't courtesy of this traitor? A set up?" Tobias asked.

Dallas shook his head and spoke with confidence. "Nope. Not a chance. Apparently, we've got our *own* secret weapon, some kid from the east coast. An old friend recruited him right after they were all released from the Damascus Facility. They talked him into joining Sebastian's ranks, posing as a supporter."

"*What* kid?" My brow tensed with the question, trying to imagine even *one* I thought capable of a task that big, that *important*. None came to mind.

Dallas shrugged. "Beats me. He didn't give a name. Not even the Elders know about this," he added. "I suppose you could say my source has trust issues when it comes to depending on the higher-ups."

I didn't like it—that there were still so many secrets, so many factors we weren't aware of.

"Why there?" Kyle asked. "Why set up camp in Ridge Borough of all places?"

Turning, I spotted beads of sweat forming on his brow.

Dallas noticed, too and asked, "Scared, pal?" He was still sporting a wide grin.

Instead of denying that there might have been truth to Dallas' accusation, Kyle owned his feelings.

"Just seems like with all this talk of traitors and secret plans, one of us needed to say it out loud."

Dallas, shaking his head, decided to ease Kyle's mind. "As a military man myself, Ridge Borough is *exactly* where I'd set up camp if I was Sebastian," he explained. "It's both close enough and far enough away from Seaton Falls to carry out whatever plans he might have. Plus, it's nestled right up against the Canadian border, which puts him at an advantage if any refugees fleeing their clans try to align with the Council to fight for the other side."

Dallas' rationale seemed to set Kyle's mind at ease.

"Am I the only one thinking we should do more than just spectate tonight?" Ivan asked. His stiff posture oozed discontentment. His expression, too.

"What would you have us do?" Declan asked with a sigh. "Rush in like brutes and sabotage our one opportunity to understand the Sovereign's plan?"

Ivan never answered, probably because he already knew why jumping the gun was a bad idea.

"We must be smart about this," Declan reasoned. "Yes, one day soon, Sebastian will get what he deserves, but we have to accept that that day has yet to arrive."

I sympathized with Ivan, but with so much riding on our success ... this plan couldn't be rushed. Now more than ever, with so much uncertainty, we had to proceed with caution.

The lives of our loved ones depended on it.

CHAPTER 4

Liam

Our drive came to an end and we trekked the rest of the way on foot. We couldn't risk the sound of Richie's engine tipping off the soldiers. With Ridge Borough being relatively small, and completely abandoned, it wasn't hard to spot activity from a good distance away.

Light coming from a rundown warehouse was the first sign of life, and then the unmarked trucks parked outside it.

This was definitely the right place, but what went on in this one building seemed to be it. None of the others were lit. No sign of an army. No sign of Sebastian, Blaise. This looked more like a skeleton crew.

We stayed low, keeping our eyes focused on the few bodies that filed in and out of the building, each hauling material back inside like an assembly line—large metal rods, huge panes of glass framed in steel, clear hoses, vats of thick, silver liquid sloshing inside transparent cylinders. Dallas passed a questioning glance my way when we spotted the first. And even now, after they'd taken in fifty or more, we were still no closer to figuring out what the substance was.

I did, however, know the name of the stones they lugged in next. They were large, so large the soldiers could only carry one at a time. Their dark blue color and iridescent outer layer made them easy to classify—Biremede stones.

They were used by witches for a number of spells, which made it hard to narrow down what Sebastian had in mind, but it was worth noting. Maybe Hilda would have answers.

We stared on as more clear barrels were hauled inside. Only three this time, but the liquid inside wasn't silver. It was red.

"Blood," Ivan sighed.

"Think it's for the witches?" Kyle asked. "We're not sure how many he has and without the lycan blood, they'll die, right?"

"Yeah, but that doesn't make sense," Richie chimed in. "The soldiers are likely providing the witches with more than enough to live off of."

"Being honest," Ben added, "*none* of this looks right."

I couldn't have agreed more.

Dallas crouched a bit lower. "Yeah, something's definitely off," he grumbled.

"And am I the only one who thought there'd be more of them?" Kyle asked, prompting several others to agree, including me. Things were far too quiet. It didn't seem like we'd been given bad info, but maybe our timing was off.

"They're clearly up to something, but there's no way Sebastian's here." Richie's tone mirrored the concern in his expression as he scanned the same scene we all did.

"What could they be planning to do with all these materials?" Ethan asked, seeming to speak for each of his brothers.

They may have been the most confused of all. I was certain

they expected to see Sebastian behaving as irrationally as he had in the past. However, they missed the many centuries he spent honing his resources, training his army to behave like a hive, functioning with one mind.

A killing machine.

Ivan breathed a deep, frustrated sigh. "Should we come back in a day or two? Would we see more?"

I stared on as I thought, eventually responding.

"No. The more often we come back, the more likely we are to get caught. Already, as it stands, if they scan these woods soon after we're gone, they'll still pick up on our scent. Coming back a second time would only mean they'd be ready for us," I replied.

Richie nodded when our thoughts aligned. "So, our only option is to get the evidence we can now," he suggested.

Usually, he seemed to be one of the more levelheaded alphas I'd come across. However, when I turned to see why he'd gone quiet, there was a look behind his eyes that let me know something in him might be changing, might be growing tired of always taking the high road.

This, too, we had in common.

"We need to get in there," he blurted. "I counted about twenty or so lycans. We're eleven strong—three lycans, six hybrids, and two dragons." He paused to glance at all of us, before adding, "I think we can take them."

"Take them?" The question came from Ben, wearing a look of disbelief following his brother's statement. "For what purpose, exactly?"

Richie didn't hesitate to explain himself, staring his brother in the eyes.

"We didn't come here just to report back that we have no idea where the Sovereign is, that we saw a few soldiers carrying in a strange liquid we can't identify, barrels of blood for a purpose we're unsure of, for an attack going down who-knows-when."

There was no missing his exasperated tone. I'd been right about him. He *was* tired of our side, the *good* side, always coming up short. It was time we got a win.

"I'm with him," I stepped up, knowing everyone might not agree, but I was certain there would be at least six who did.

"We're with you." Declan spoke for himself and the rest of his brothers. This thought was only confirmed when they stood as well, abandoning the position where we once hid out of sight.

Richie gave a nod and the other three stood—those of our group who weren't nearly as sure as the rest of us.

"Then, I guess we're doing this," Dallas groaned, his heavy, Southern drawl elongating the syllables. The sound of which made his disdain for this leg of our plan abundantly clear.

Richie sprang right into action once everyone was on board. "Good, so half of us will come in from the east, the other half from the west. We'll surround the building and close in on them. Once we have eyes on the soldiers, we take them out one by one, as silently as possible to avoid making ourselves anymore obvious than we need to."

"And what, pray tell, do you suggest we do next?" Dallas inquired, doing little to hide the irritation in his tone. "Tie 'em up and interrogate 'em?"

I shook my head, answering for Richie. "Nope. They'll never talk. All we need are samples to get to Hilda. If anyone knows what this stuff is for, it's her."

With the grin that spread across Caleb's face, I guessed he liked where this plan was headed, liked that we didn't need to be careful to spare any lives. We may have all been a bit eager to get our hands dirty for a change.

"We'll go east," he volunteered, pointing at himself and his brothers.

"Then, west it is," Richie countered, just before we split into our *own* group—him, Ben, Kyle, Dallas, and me.

These woods were dark. Darker than those surrounding Seaton Falls. With this town practically being dead, there was no residual light illuminating the sky. Only the striking contrast between the void of space and the intense glow of its stars.

The closer we got to our mark, the more my body pulsed with anticipation. My fists filled with heat and faint, red light pulsed through them.

Red.

It was new, very different from the usual pale orange I was used to from my dragon. And this wasn't the *only* change. The day I forced Elise's hand, made certain she had no choice but to reanimate me, I was … *different*. I felt it.

Felt the power beneath my wings that now spanned nearly twice their normal width, moving air in powerful gusts.

Felt it in my entire body that was now unmistakably larger when in my shifted form.

Felt it in the white-hot rage that swelled within me.

The change left me feeling as though I no longer knew myself, my dragon. It was still part of me, only now, it was a part of me I wasn't quite familiar with yet.

One of Elise's main concerns was that, by me already having genetic dragon DNA within my cells, when she turned me I'd change in ways none of us could predict. I suppose she'd been right about that part. While I still had a lot to understand, I was certain of one thing.

I was better off this way.

And I'd do it all over again if it came down to it.

"Something's up ahead," Dallas whispered.

Our steps halted at his words. I scanned until I spotted it, too—two figures beside a window on the first floor of the warehouse. Not too far from where they stood, an open door to a second loading bay provided us with a point of entry.

"That's our way in," Richie decided, speaking my thoughts aloud. "I'll lure them out and—"

"And I'll take it from there," I interjected.

More heat surged through my forearms and fists, as I anticipated the opportunity to give Sebastian's men exactly what they deserved.

Richie didn't argue. As soon as we reached an understanding, we filed out. He made quick work of moving toward the entrance and, tossing a small stone against the aluminum siding of the warehouse, the two lycans we had our sights on showed themselves.

They assessed Richie, scanned to gage whether he was alone. I knew the instant they caught my scent from around the corner. One pivoted on his heel, but I was on them *both* in an instant, cinching their throats as my forearms forced out their last breath. I left them no time to call out to the other soldiers, no time to shift, or react at *all* for that matter. We had to make this quick and clean.

The last sputters of air left the guards' mouths. They seemed so frail. Both bodies slumped to the ground and gashes in my skin slowly healed where their nails had torn into it. They did their best to claw their way out of my grasp, but it simply wasn't enough.

"The others should be moving in on the other side by now," Dallas whispered, keeping his back flush against the siding. We still had to maintain a low profile until we brought their numbers down to match ours.

"Three at the top of the stairs," Kyle breathed, settling his head back again after the brief glimpse inside.

"We'll wait for them to come down, then strike," Ben whispered back.

A nod confirmed this as our plan and we waited, listening as soft-soled shoes thudded against the metal steps.

"Sounds like all three," Dallas confirmed. "Two heading this way, one toward the east entrance."

"I've got one this time," Kyle volunteered, not bothering to hide how much he looked forward to it.

"I'll take the other," Ben offered, sounding far less enthusiastic than his brother a moment before.

Luckily, they were heading out toward us without being coaxed. It meant we didn't have to give away our positions to lure them. No one breathed. We stood like statues against the building as the pair of shadows came closer. When it was time to act, Kyle nodded to Ben and the two made quick work of wrangling the soldiers to the ground.

Kyle had choked his mark out cold within seconds, but Ben hadn't gotten as good a grip. The lycan he chose dragged his feet through the dirt and gravel, making more noise than any of us wanted. Things would have been so much easier if we were able to sneak in undetected.

...Would have been.

"They've got us surrounded," a voice called out, alerting fifteen or more of our presence.

With the notion of coming in quietly now out the window, we stormed in.

The strange, red flames burst from within when my dragon broke free. My senses had always been sharp, but were even more so now. It was as if I heard and saw things half a second before they actually happened.

A lycan rushed me from the left. I not only saw him, but felt a shift in the air currents that moved over my skin as he barreled forward. I was completely aware of him, but never directed an ounce of attention his way. My eyes stayed trained on the situation unfolding around me as my hand shot toward the soldier's neck, coiling his body toward mine like a serpent.

The swift motion seemed to catch him off guard. Needing to end him so I could move on to the next. My chosen method was to rip his head from his shoulders.

His screams rang out through the warehouse as my fingers locked firm beneath his jaw. The feel of it ripping free from his face—soft flesh tearing, bone separating from bone—it only fed the beast within me.

Only made me hungry for more.

Writhing in pain, he hit the ground. There was no time to watch him bleed out, so I silenced his groans a moment later, crushing his skull beneath my boot. Blood sprayed up, covering my neck and face, but another charged toward me before a breath could even leave my mouth. However, to his surprise, I was ready for him. His full sprint came to a sudden halt, and after being slammed to the ground, his gaze was now locked on the ceiling. He could hardly get a breath of air into his lungs, but that was to be expected seeing as how his heart was no longer inside his chest.

He stared at my fist as I held it above him, possibly reflecting on how things played out. Intent on ending *my* life, the tables had quickly turned.

Streams of blood rushed toward my elbow and I made certain the image that carried him into death was that of his life source beating in the palm of my hand. When his eyes went vacant, I dropped the hunk of meat back inside his chest and moved on.

This experience ... was different. The energy that fed my dragon was mine, but ... not. It was hard to explain, but I felt it without a doubt. It was stronger, more focused.

More vicious.

Without thought, I laid down five more, freeing arms and limbs from bodies, tossing them into a growing heap behind me. Before long, the commotion that had suddenly roared to life around us, lulled to the muffled whimper of one soldier as Dallas snapped his spine in two.

We stood surveying as we caught our breath, counting bodies, losing track because most were in pieces.

"Well, I believe that's everyone." All eyes went to Josiah when he spoke.

We were all pretty sure that was the case. After one last scan, I pulled my shirt over my head. Unlike the blood-slathered front, the back was mostly stain-free. I used it to wipe myself somewhat clean, but mostly just smeared lycan blood all over myself.

It was a slight improvement, though.

Slight.

Beside me, Richie sighed before speaking. "Now to figure out which one has the keys to that truck outside."

My gaze shifted toward him. "Is this a new plan?" I asked.

He shrugged, following my lead as he removed his shirt to wipe a mixture of blood and sweat from his face. "Not necessarily. Just seems counterproductive to leave them with all their supplies. My guess is others will be arriving by no later than morning to start building … whatever this is," he said, gesturing toward the large, steel-framed glass we watch them lug in.

Ben chimed in next. "They can't build what they don't have."

"And what they don't build, they can't use against us," Dallas added.

Richie nodded, realizing we'd begun to see the logic. "Exactly. So, let's find these keys so we—"

There was a sound.

One I heard half a second before spotting the source … a dark object that cut through the air, streaking across the warehouse at warp speed. What came next was a deep, primitive roar that ricocheted off the aluminum walls that surrounded us.

Ivan's body slumped to the ground and it was second nature for his brothers and me to shield him with our own. He'd been hit with an arrow.

There was no sign of the attacker, so with a second to assess Ivan's condition, where he'd been hit, I glanced back. The puncture wound had just begun to ooze, but what stood out even more was how it sizzled around the metal shaft. I could only guess the agony it caused as Ivan grunted, gritted his teeth so loudly it rivaled the volume of his roar. This was no ordinary arrow.

Something wasn't right.

"It's just his shoulder," Declan observed, only turning toward Ivan a second before scanning for the perpetrator again. I noted the angle from which the arrow had been released.

Second level balcony. Right over the railing

"Keep an eye on him," I called out, sprinting toward the steps, leaping over two and three at a time.

Whoever had done this, whoever thought it wise to injure one of my brothers ... they'd pay.

It was hard to hear over the sound of Ivan's voice when he yelled out. It bounced off the hard, metallic surfaces and back again, seeming to come from everywhere. Unable to rely on sound, I leaned heavier on my other senses.

Dragons weren't known for their sense of smell, but unfortunately for *this* guy, mine had become keener in the last twenty-four-hours. The scent of sweat and fear filled my nostrils when I breathed deep, pinpointing exactly where to find him. I bounded across the metal grates that linked together to form the floor. When I sent a steel barrel flying over the rail, down to the lower level, I had the bastard's full attention.

He'd chosen the wrong day to be brave. This could've all been avoided if he'd just let us leave and stayed hidden.

But now, his pride was about to cost him his life.

He wasn't ready to give up. I knew as much when his biceps swelled and burst through the sleeves of his shirt. I had him off the ground and hoisted in the air before he realized shifting was now too little too late. Doing so would only make killing him more interesting, but it wouldn't stop me.

He'd nearly finished transforming into his wolf when I brought his weight down from where I held him above my head, aligning the center of his mass with my knee.

The crunch of his vertebrae brought an end to the struggle. I tossed him aside, but stopped before rushing down to check in on Ivan who seemed to be in even more pain now than when he was first hit.

I needed an arrow, one to take back to Hilda to analyze and fix whatever had just been done to Ivan. If it was as I suspected, if we were going to assess whether it *was* in fact laced with magic, having one in our possession was imperative.

Pulling one of the two from the dead lycan's quiver, I rushed down to Ivan's side. Declan peered up as he held his brother's hand through the agony.

"I removed the shaft, but he's not healing," he uttered with a shaken voice.

"We have to get him back. Fast," I called out.

"Found the keys," Kyle piped, pulling them from the pocket of a dead lycan.

Declan, Caleb, Ethan, and I carried Ivan to the truck while the others made quick work of loading the supplies we agreed should be taken off Sebastian's hands.

Tonight was mostly a success, but as I watched my brother writhing in pain, uncertain what lie ahead for him, I was left to wonder ... *had it been worth the cost?*

CHAPTER 5

Evie

It was him.
I'd know that face, his presence, *anywhere.*

Frozen in time, Liam stood in the doorway of a room I didn't recognize. One I felt I knew despite never having been in this place. Stone walls with evenly spaced torches mounted, casting odd shadows.

The familiarity of it all was both unsettling and a comfort.

I was aware it was night even before turning to face the terrace —an open space framed with pillars and ivory-colored sheers that billowed in the breeze. Beyond it, an inky abyss dotted with twinkling stars held my undivided attention.

Until he said my name.

"...Evangeline."

I turned toward him then, feeling emotions I didn't understand —anger ... lust.

That one, in particular, I seemed to be resisting most.

Both arms crossed my chest as I stared in defiance, but never spoke.

My lack of response made him smirk, a devilish grin that rested on his lips as he scanned the length of me. It was a sweeping look that dragged up my bare leg that peeped out from a slit in a thin, white garment, to my waist cinched by a brown, leather strip, to my chest where the material crossed before tying around my neck.

Where was I?

Or ... when was I?

His clothing stood out to me now, too—a top with loose sleeves that hid the defined muscle just beneath them, dark pants that clung to toned thighs before disappearing inside boots the same shade.

I looked him over much like he'd done to me. The buttons of his shirt were undone, and my gaze lingered there, on the rolling hills of a tight abdomen I could practically feel against my palms.

Time seemed relative in this bizarre trance, or ... dream maybe. I recalled drifting off while awaiting an update from Liam while he and the guys followed the lead to Ridge Borough, but this didn't quite feel like a dream.

It felt real.

Two words left Liam's mouth and I gave him every ounce of my attention. "Forgive me."

I blinked, swallowed hard, blinked again.

"My behavior tonight was inexcusable. I saw him touch you and ... I lost myself," he admitted, fondling the point of a blade holstered at his hip.

I continued to bridle my tongue, finding these circumstances vaguely familiar. Like ... déjà vu.

"It's my sworn duty to protect you," he went on, "both physically and in reputation."

I scoffed when he finished. "And, in your opinion, being kissed by the son of a duke would mar my reputation? Better yet, striking him was a sensible solution?"

The sound of my voice startled me because these were not my thoughts. It was as if I sat off to the side listening to a recording despite feeling present.

The sudden tension in Liam's brow made it obvious my cynicism irritated him.

"I said ... I apologize," he muttered slowly.

Ignoring his attempt at smoothing over what I guessed to be a disagreement, I spoke to him sharply.

"You had no right! What I do, nor whom I do it with, are any of your concern."

He chuckled, finding something I said amusing.

"I didn't come here to argue," he insisted. As soon as the words left his mouth, he turned to leave.

A strange mix of frustration and desperation filled me, and I took a step in his direction. Then, a question left my mouth. "Why?"

That simple phrase halted his steps, but he didn't turn again to face me. Instead, I was left to stare at broad shoulders that heaved as he lingered in the narrow corridor.

"Why what?" he countered.

"Why do you ... care?" My voice quaked and I was certain he heard it, too.

With each breath, my chest strained against the material that sparsely covered it. Inside, my heart hammered a mile a minute and all I could think as I watched him was ... don't go.

The words never came out, but they were felt.

"I thought I already made this clear," Liam seethed. "I stopped him because protecting you is my duty," he reasoned. "It's what I do."

Defiance rose within me and I couldn't fight the urge to push—

to push him to the edge where he'd have to say more, would have to say the words I didn't have the courage to admit myself.

"Your duty? And nothing else?"

He stood in silence a moment before turning to face me as he replied. "What more would you like to hear, Evangeline?"

"The truth." My swift response rendered him speechless.

Heavy steps echoed against the stone walls and high ceiling when he came closer, his gaze never leaving me when he spoke.

"There's nothing more to say. Nothing you don't already know if you're honest with yourself," he accused.

We were so close now. Close enough that heat from his skin danced over my own.

"I'm in love with you," he blurted, no sign of fear or waning confidence in sight as he said more. "I've always loved you."

A breath hitched in my throat as his advancing steps caused me to take several back into the room I'd been coaxed out of by desperation.

Desperation to stop him from leaving.

Desperation to hear him say these very words.

That breath I held breezed over my lips when large hands took my waist, making it impossible to escape him.

"So, forgive me," he repeated. "Forgive me for falling in love and not being able to stand the sight of you with another man."

Hearing him speak his truth, like a man with nothing to lose, I knew that was exactly how he felt. He had nothing to lose and everything to gain.

Me.

My heart—something I was certain he had long before I willingly admitted it.

Without a second thought, I allowed him to enter the room, knowing what he'd expect if I latched the heavy, wooden door behind him. However, I did it anyway, because his assumptions would have been accurate.

This strange space between reality and fiction felt like we owned it. Only us. No one else.

Smooth skin met my fingers when I moved them beneath the lapel of his shirt, pushing the material down his shoulders and arms until it fell to the floor. There, dark ink covered his skin, confirming what I already knew. This wasn't real. Couldn't have been. Those markings were erased when Elise resurrected him, but ...

As my fingers moved over the curves and sharp edges of symbols etched in my memory, it certainly felt real.

A soft kiss pressed to my lips and I kissed him back, my eyes staying open as I stared, finding it hard to believe he had the audacity to touch me like this. Finding it hard to believe I dared to let him.

Those lips moved to my neck, causing heat to scatter everywhere—up my back, my legs ... all over. The room went dark when the relief of finally giving in forced my eyes closed. Each step we took toward the bed was a reminder of the many reasons we should have resisted one another, why I should have let him walk away when he tried.

"What if Father finds out?"

The concern escaped my lips as a breathy sigh when the fabric against my chest loosened, and then fell away. The next thing that touched my flesh was his—two warm palms, anxious fingers.

I'd nearly forgotten my own question when Liam answered it.

"There's still time to stop," he crooned against my ear. "... if that's what you want."

The response was almost laughable as he tugged the belt free from my waist, flinging it carelessly as I brought him down on top of me—the softness of me pressed against the never-ending firmness of him. The mattress cradled us, and our want for one another nearly swallowed us whole.

He was all heat and passion. From head to toe. Even the

lingering fear of being caught wasn't enough to stop things from moving forward.

What if someone came looking for us?

What if they heard us?

Those concerns, and any that followed, evaporated around us like the steam rolling off our now-naked bodies. Flames threatened to blaze bright just beneath the surface of our skin, but we held it in, dispersing the unvented aggression in other ways.

At the thought, a firm grip seized my hip and the rough motion brought a satisfied smile to my lips. The next second ... I was his, being claimed by my warrior for the first time.

I panted unashamedly as his rhythm, the power behind his every move, took my breath away. Despite a vehement effort to control myself, his name lingered on the tip of my tongue, and finally slipped from my lips to his ears. The sound of which stoking the passion between us.

Where my hands stretched above, gripping his chest, embers glowed just beneath them where we fought to contain our flames. Our dragons had responded in kind as our physical bodies connected, forming an intimate bond that ran deeper than any words could ever express. This act of passion proved something. Something I hadn't questioned in a long time.

Every bit of who I was belonged to him.

―――

Gentle kisses to my forehead, cheek, and finally my lips roused me awake.

"Morning, beautiful."

That deep, melodic voice made me grin and I hadn't even opened my eyes yet.

Half dazed, I blinked sleepily into his hazel stare, that handsomely rugged face I'd just seen in a dream. It comforted me through the night while he'd been away on a mission with my brothers, Dallas.

"I missed you," I groaned, inching closer for another kiss. He returned it with two more. Remnants of the night's fantasy still left my heart racing just being close to him now, and I guessed it would for a while.

Wet hair and fresh clothes meant he showered before waking me. I'd been worried sick about him, but wanted him to think I hadn't let my nerves get the best of me. I didn't like the idea of them being out there all night, chasing after the Sovereign but understood.

From what I could see, Liam was unharmed. Or, at least whatever injuries he *did* have were healed now. Still, I didn't want to think about that, him getting hurt.

He seemed ... distant, like his mind was elsewhere. At the feel of my hand against his cheek his wandering gaze settled on me.

"What is it?" I asked quietly, doing my best to hide the fear I felt in regards to what his answer might be.

When it took him a moment to respond, I knew. Knew something had gone wrong.

" ... Liam."

He looked away, this time not bothering to pretend everything was okay.

"You can't get worked up," he said in the most soothing voice he could manage. "We have to be careful of that now, in your condition," he clarified.

The warning only made things worse, only made me *more* certain things hadn't quite gone according to plan.

"It's ... Ivan," he revealed, causing my heart to sink. "Before you panic, he's alive, but ... that's about *all* we know for now."

I didn't understand. "But I thought this was just recon? Why were *any* of you close enough for something like this to happen?"

"We moved in to get a better look around, to get more information," was Liam's explanation.

I sat up to focus. Sure, I worried a bit before falling asleep, but I was mildly comforted thinking last night was all about observation. Now, to hear they'd come face-to-face with someone from Sebastian's camp?

And what Elise must be going through ...

What *Liam* must be going through.

My hand went to his cheek and I was relieved to see he wasn't hiding his emotions. I was sure, had anyone else been in the room, he would have concealed them. But he knew he could share anything with me.

"Are you okay?" I asked, despite knowing it was a stupid question. Of *course* he wasn't okay.

"I'm trying to be," he replied, giving the most honest answer he could.

I was terrified for Ivan, but it wasn't lost on me that there was a difference between *my* bond with him, versus his with Liam. I cared, and there was an immediate sense of love and loyalty I felt toward Ivan and *all* my brothers, but ... this was all new. Their connection with Liam had withstood the test of time. It was solid.

Deep.

I could only imagine how this was affecting them.

"I'd like to see him," I stated, sitting up in bed, pausing when Liam took a light hold of my wrist.

"I don't think that's wise," he urged. "Ivan's not ... he's not well. Had Hilda not sedated him, he'd still be out of his mind with pain, but still ... there's nothing she can do about the wound."

That agony I sensed from the beginning was more apparent now, but I was suspicious he didn't just feel it for himself. Maybe he felt it for me, too. Maybe he was *also* reminded of a time not so long ago when I sat by *his* side while he lie in a similar state. At the thought of it—how desperate and dark those days were for me—I shuddered.

Pushing the horrible memory aside, my gaze locked with his. "I'll be fine," I insisted, placing a foot on the carpet.

He was one step ahead of me, hopping up to approach my side of the bed in the blink of an eye.

"Evangeline, stress is the last thing you need right now. The others all agree," he reasoned, placing both hands on my waist as he drew me closer.

I guessed he thought he could stop me, but his plea went in one ear and out the other. I was pretty sure my family was struggling to hold it together just beyond this bedroom door and I intended to help in whatever way I could. Staying locked in here wasn't an option. I wasn't an invalid, wasn't fragile. Not *yet* anyway. Heck, just yesterday none of us even knew there was anything going on with me. I wouldn't start acting helpless twenty-four-hours later simply because I was now aware of my condition.

"I'm fine," I assured him with a kiss to his cheek.

He stared when I slipped from his grasp to change out of my nightshirt and into a tee and shorts. I was ready to head out, but a pleading stare halted me.

"He's in a bad way, Evangeline ... Please."

It was then, when he all but begged me not to go to Ivan right away, that I knew for sure he meant to protect me from my own memories, from what I'd been through.

As much as I wanted to be at my brother's side, as much as I wanted to show my support to the others, I wouldn't push. I'd been stubborn and defiant enough in recent weeks for a lifetime. I'd give Liam a break on this one and would wait to visit Ivan at a better time.

"Okay," I finally conceded.

Liam was visibly relieved when I caved. Immediately, tension drained from his expression and he breathed easier.

"Where's Elise?" I asked, moving toward the bed to sit again before adding, "Is she holding up okay?"

He took slow steps away from the door as he thought of how to answer.

"She's ... strong, of course, but I think it'd be good if you checked in on her. Seeing him like this hasn't been easy," he answered.

I figured as much. She must have been devastated. After everything she'd gone through to bring them back. To bring *us* back.

"I'll go check on her, but please tell my brothers my heart is with them," I requested. If I couldn't stand at their side, I at least wanted them to know I was beside them in spirit.

Liam gave a nod. "I will, but keeping you away wasn't just my idea. It was theirs, too."

Of course it was. Knowing how much they cared about me, *loved* me ... it brought a smile to my face.

Since meeting them, not a day went by that I wasn't reminded of how important they were to me, to our unit as a whole. Now with one wounded, it was like holding my breath, hoping and praying Ivan would pull through.

Whatever happened from here ... it was happening to all of us.

My family.

CHAPTER 6

Evie

I stood outside Elise's bedroom, waiting. From what Liam explained, she'd been at Ivan's side since they arrived home at the crack of dawn. Had it not been for Hilda insisting she get some rest, I was certain she'd still be there.

Quiet steps on the other side of the door had me standing straighter. With all that transpired, there was no telling what state I'd find her in. There was already so much resting on our shoulders collectively as a family, and now this situation with Ivan.

Elise opened up and, right away, her gaze turned watery, as if she'd been holding it all in until this very moment. There were a number of things I could have said, but every word eluded me and all I could think to do was hug her.

My arms went around her neck and the emotions she kept hidden came rushing out like a flood.

" ... I wish I could fix it," I whispered as we embraced.

It was true. If I could have taken all these bad things away and given her the one thing she always wanted, no strings attached, I would have in a heartbeat. Her heart and intentions were so pure. Nothing would have made her happier than to have a normal life without worrying it'd all be taken away from her in the blink of an eye.

On that point, we were of the same mind.

"Where are my manners," she sniffled. "Come in."

I followed her inside and the door was latched behind me. She made her way across the room to her bed where I was invited to take a seat on the lavish, champagne-colored duvet. Cool silk met my fingertips when I eased down onto it.

Long lashes blinked over Elise's eyes as she searched for words.

"How's Liam?" she asked, not surprising me in the least. She was the embodiment of the word 'mother', always thinking of our wellbeing before her own.

"Fine," I assured her. "He went back up to Hilda's workroom to be with Ivan and the others."

That seemed to be the response she expected.

"You'll have to forgive me," she began, her voice quiet and strained. "I know you're probably here to discuss Ivan's condition, but ... if you don't mind, I'd rather not. My heart's just ... it's so heavy," she admitted. "Having just come through this with Liam, I ..."

Her voice trailed off and I understood completely, because I felt the same. We'd just watched another loved one fight for his life and these circumstances were too fresh, her emotions too raw.

I offered a dim smile. "Then we'll talk about something else. *Anything* else. You pick."

Her dark hair shifted over her shoulder with a nod. "Well, to start, how are you feeling?" she asked. "There's been a lot to take in in a short amount of time. How are you coping with ... your news?" she said next.

Right away, I felt self-conscious. What an idiot she must have thought I was. Because, being honest, I'd already been thinking it myself. I mean, I had *no clue* what was going on with my own body until Nick made it abundantly clear.

Because of this, I wasn't sure how to answer. My condition made us more vulnerable as a unit. Everyone would, no doubt, be hyper-vigilant when it came to keeping me safe.

Maybe at the expense of others.

Maybe at the expense of themselves.

There was nothing I could do to change that. Even centuries apart from my brothers hadn't lessened the fact that I was still their sister and they would always regard me as such.

I locked eyes with Elise and replied, "I'm ... fine."

I had such a way with words.

Taking a deep breath, I said more. "I'm sorry about how this could affect everyone. It was stupid, I know." My palm pressed to my forehead when I went on. "Liam and I should have been more careful under the circumstances. We were just swept up in our emotions, I guess. Nearly losing one another may have clouded our judgment and we weren't thinking and..."

My rambling was cut short when Elise all but snatched me into another embrace, one so tight and heartfelt I knew I'd been wrong.

"Evangeline ... this child is the miracle we all need right now. A light in a world filled with darkness."

At those words, my smile stretched wider. She hadn't been thinking *any* of those terrible things. As usual, nothing but love emanated from within her, transferring to me the longer she held on. I quickly realized how much I needed this, a hug from her.

My mother.

It was beginning to feel less strange thinking of her in that light, as the one who'd given me life. *Twice,* at that. For so long, I kept her at arm's length, clinging to the idea that I could only ever have regarded one woman as *'Mom'*—Rebecka Callahan. However, the more I was able to see Elise's heart and realize the depth of her love, the easier it became to accept her role in my life.

My arms cinched tighter around her, and I exhaled with relief.

"You could not have made me happier," she added to her already kind statement. Her eyes gleamed even more when sharing her next thought. "We've got so much to prepare for. So much to *buy*."

I could only imagine how much she intended to spend *'preparing'*. The woman certainly had a penchant for shopping.

When I leaned away and let my gaze sync with hers, I shook my head.

"You don't have to do anything," I insisted. "Our hands are already full. Besides, we've still got what ... nearly seven or eight months to worry about all that?"

A perfectly arched brow quirked when I finished speaking, and then Elise's reply only confused me.

"Seven or eight? Evangeline, you ..."

She paused and studied my bewildered expression for a moment.

"I think it might be a good idea for me to share something with you. Something that might help you gain a better understanding," she suggested.

I still wasn't sure what about the comment grabbed her attention, but then she laid it all out on the table and, suddenly, it made sense.

Well ... sort of.

"The gestation period for a lycan is nine months, but ... you're not just a lycan. You're part dragon, too, so ... the time could be *slightly* shorter than what you may be thinking."

A warm hand came down on top of mine and I stared at her.

"Wait ... you said *'could be'* slightly shorter, as in you're not sure? And just how much shorter are we talking?" An abrupt, cynical laugh slipped out behind the question. Mostly, it was nerves.

"Well, I worded it this way because, quite frankly, by you being a hybrid ... it could go either way. Only time will tell and it's up to your body to decide," she admitted, causing all expression to leave my face.

She took note of the look and went on to explain further. "If a female dragon has chosen to assimilate herself into a human community, she pretends to have been expecting much longer than her actual experience. It would be her only cover," she added.

I got the feeling this was a stall tactic, Elise's way of biding her time before having to lay the cold, hard truth on me.

"For instance," she went on, "a woman in this situation may tell her close human friends she simply withheld the news of her pregnancy until it's nearly over. Until she's crested."

I'd never heard the term used in this context, so I asked for clarity. " ... Crested? What's that mean?"

Elise nodded and the slight hesitation in her tone wasn't lost on me.

"Well, the literal definition that applies here is that it's a peak. Like the top of a mountain, or wave," she explained. "For you, should your body decide to follow the path of a dragon, cresting will be the peak of the pregnancy, the midway point. At which time it will no longer be possible to hide that you're with child." She paused to give me a moment to process it all before adding something else.

"It will also be the beginning of an intense bonding experience between you and your child, one only understood by another drag-on," After explaining, I watched as a distant smile graced her lips and her thoughts seemed to drift a bit, maybe recalling her own experiences.

"What's it like?"

Dark, gentle eyes peered up when I asked.

"It's beautiful," she laughed—a light, girlish sound that matched her youthful appearance. "However, it can also be quite challenging ... *physically*. With how quickly the child will begin to grow from this point, your body may find it difficult to cope at first, but that's when it's important to remember that many dragons before you endured the discomfort and survived. Becoming a mother will change you, Evangeline. In ways you could never even imagine. There's something about needing to protect your child that brings out who you really are, what you're truly made of."

She paused and a warm smile followed.

I nodded, imagining that to be true, noting all the sacrifices she'd made for my brothers and I, the hard choices she's made through the years. The weight of our conversation must have been why she steered it back toward our original path.

"But as I was saying, the reason female dragons wait until they've crested to reveal their condition to the outside world is to avoid raising red flags."

I asked my question again. "How much shorter would it be for me if I ..."

Elise gripped my hand just a little tighter when fear made the sentence trail off. Her attempt at soothing me might have worked had the answer she gave a moment later not been so starkly different from what I prepared for.

Seven months? Six maybe?

"You'll be... It's..." She stammered before finally blurting it. "Three months."

That answer ... it drew every ounce of air right out of the room. My eyes stretched wide before blinking more than what felt natural in the few seconds it took to realize I hadn't misheard.

"Th ... three? But I've already surpassed the first month," I stuttered.

Meaning, three months could now be two, inching danger-ously close to one.

A sympathetic hug went around my shoulders. "I know this is all a lot to take in, but you're more than capable of handling it," she assured me once again.

My reaction had less to do with whether I was physically suited for the task, and more to do with the state of our lives. If I had a more reasonable stretch of time before I was at my most defenseless, I could have been of some use in this fight. However, if this 'cresting' Elise spoke of were to actually happen to me, it was only a couple weeks away. If that time came, if my body sided with my dragon, I wouldn't be any good to *anyone*.

I'd be a liability.

My family's Achilles heel.

"I was afraid you'd panic," Elise whispered when I did just that. Panicked.

Frantic tears threatened to fall and I felt my heart beating triple time.

"There's just ... so much to figure out," I panted. "So much to get straight before the..." I couldn't even say the word.

Baby—there was so much to get straight before the baby got here.

Just thinking it now, knowing how quick this process could be, I was overcome with dread. Saying that word out loud would have made it real, would force me to face the fact that the timing of it all couldn't have been worse.

A foreign instinct jolted me, one I neither invited nor welcomed. It was brought on by the acknowledgement that this world we lived in was too unstable for deep connections—like the one formed between mother and child. It all felt like one big, cruel joke—to be immortal, and yet so finite. The little one I carried ... he or she only made an already bitter pill that much more difficult to swallow.

I didn't want to love anyone else. Not when losing that love was such a great possibility. But I knew those feelings for him or her would come regardless of whether I welcomed them or not. And when they did, I also knew it would be unlike anything else I'd ever known.

"Evangeline?"

Hearing my name pulled me from my thoughts to meet Elise's stare. When I did, it became clear our deep conversation about life and motherhood was about to take a sharp turn.

"I've been thinking," she blurted. "Especially with what's gone on with Ivan, with how quickly things can go terribly wrong," she rambled. "And ... you can't stay here. It's imperative that we get you someplace safe."

My eyes stretched wide with her suggestion.

"Now you sound like Liam," I remarked.

"That doesn't surprise me. He's always been wise, intuitive when it comes to looking after you," she replied.

I breathed deep, wondering if *anyone* was on my side when it came to how I saw things.

"Next thing I know, you'll suggest I be assigned a ... *keeper*," I sighed. "Which is basically just a glorified babysitter."

"They were common in days past. I, myself, was assigned one, but traded her for Hilda," Elise shared. "While that's not the worst idea in the world, having someone watch over you still wouldn't be as effective as taking you someplace safe."

"And leave you all to act as some sacrificial firewall when Sebastian storms this place looking for me?" I shot back.

"Hilda already placed more sigils on the house, the property," she rattled off. Her posture was poised as usual when she said more. "The rest of us will do what we've always done. We'll fight, we'll survive, but we can't risk exposing you to whatever tactics Sebastian employs next," she insisted.

I kept my expression even, unreadable. "Hilda can do whatever she wants to the house, the land, but I won't leave here."

A strange sense of belonging filled me to the brim as I stood my ground. I felt downright territorial over this town I once couldn't stand the thought of calling home, but it was exactly that. My home. I wouldn't let Sebastian or anyone else run me away from it.

Elise didn't argue, but there was no missing the fearful expression she couldn't hide.

"Evangeline, it's honorable that you want to stay, that you want to stand in solidarity with your people, but ... under these circumstances, no one would think any less of you if you allowed us to take extra precautions," she insisted. "Especially for the baby's sake."

It would have been so easy to run like they suggested, so easy to use my newly discovered condition as an excuse to get away from it all, pretend none of it existed, but I didn't want that. I didn't want to sit this one out and it had nothing to do with anyone's judgement. I couldn't have cared less what others outside these four walls thought of me, my family. It came down to me not being willing to stand by while the ones I loved fell, all because they wanted to protect me.

"I might be of some help."

Elise scoffed and the reaction surprised me. "I don't think you understand. In two short weeks, this child may begin to develop quite rapidly, Evangeline," she warned, reiterating her point before letting it go. "That's only fourteen days."

When I remained silent, thinking of all the reasons to turn down Elise's suggestion just like I had when Liam made it, she took the moment of silence to say more.

"What I'm suggesting is that, for once, you think of yourself first," she pleaded, practically panting as her dark eyes watered again. "At every turn, you're darting out into danger, holding little to no regard for your own life. Only, this time, it isn't just about you," she expressed, her gaze narrowing when she asked a question. "Don't you understand the terrible turn this could take? Aren't you afraid?"

I swiped a rogue tear from my cheek before answering, feeling no shame when I admitted the truth. "Terrified, actually."

Elise gave a knowing nod before trying to reason with me again. "Then let us protect you."

I heard her loud and clear, but even letting my imagination ponder every possible tragedy, I couldn't agree.

"Being scared doesn't give me the right to run," I concluded.

Elise was silent and clearly frustrated as she stared—the rims of her dainty nostrils flaring with each breath. When she realized I wouldn't bend, she was visibly shaken—a fact that was proven when I took her hand, feeling it tremble for myself.

"I'm staying because, if I don't, if I go away like you're asking me to do, no one I leave behind will focus. Everyone's minds will be on me, worrying, but never here. Never in the fight like it should be. *Including* yours," I added, "and I can't have that on my conscience."

My voice was shaky when I told her more than I intended to. "I've already lost one mom ... I can't handle losing another."

Elise's eyes were glassy pools before eventually spilling over. However, her controlled expression never changed.

Pushing my own tears away, I forced out the last thought that ran through my head.

"I need you, Elise. Not just Liam; I need *all* of you. Everyone," I admitted, and it was true.

Each member of my family was important. Elise my comforter, Liam and my brothers the ultimate protectors, Hilda my guide, and Dallas the most level-headed person I ever met. Not a single one was expendable.

When I leaned in, Elise did what came naturally, what *any* good mother would have done—she held me, stroking my hair as every fear, every emotion I couldn't let the others know I held came spilling out.

She didn't ask questions or force me to bare more of my soul than I already had. She didn't rush me to pull it together. Even in *her* hour of grief as Ivan lie in limbo, she comforted me.

For a moment, I was allowed to forget my eventual title, allowed to forget the outside world's expectations. Sitting there with Elise, she only acknowledged *one* role I played in this life.

For now, I was just her daughter.

CHAPTER 7

Liam

Hilda scrolled from one picture to the next. Instead of taking her away from Ivan, Dallas thought photos of what we'd stolen from Sebastian the night before would suffice for now.

She paced while scanning the images, a grave expression set on her always-stoic face.

"Any initial thoughts?" Dallas asked, crossing both arms over his chest.

Her steps halted when she breathed deep.

"Biremede," she breathed, fixating on that particular photo for a while before speaking again. "There aren't many known uses for it, but I'm led to believe Sebastian may intend to commune with the Oracles, or *something* of that nature."

My brow tensed as I locked both arms across my chest. "Is that possible?"

Hilda gave a nod. "It can be done," she sighed. "If someone is not summoned directly and wishes to be heard, there is a possibility of forcing your way into their presence. A way to *make* them hear you," she explained.

Her statement trailed off as she continued to study the photo. From the look she wore, she was just as troubled as I was by the news she brought to light. Sebastian communicating with the Oracles was less than ideal. I imagined what sort of business he might have with them. Did he intend to feed them lies that would garner their sympathy and persuade them to support his cause? Was such a thing even possible with their ability to know and sense things others could not? There was just no way to tell, but what I *did* know was that we at least stalled him.

"Are you sure that's what he's planning?" I asked, noting how the question clearly frustrated Hilda. I could tell as much from the stern look she leveled on me right after.

"Perhaps you missed the part where I said I *believe* these are his intentions. I gave no guarantee," she snapped. I was no stranger to her being short-tempered on occasion, but I couldn't tiptoe around her short fuse today. I needed answers. We all did.

"I'm only asking what else you think he could have planned," I amended, being mindful to keep my tone cool. If she even *thought* I was losing my temper, she'd bite my head off again.

Trust me, I'd crossed her enough times to know. Family or not, she had no problem putting me in my place.

After a brief eye roll, it seemed we were ready to continue our conversation. However, when we did, Hilda didn't readily share whatever theories rolled around inside her head. There definitely was at least one other option, one she wasn't saying aloud.

"I'll look into it," she said dismissively, turning her attention to Ivan again when he shifted on the cot.

She'd kept a close eye on him. My gaze fell on him now, too.

He didn't look good—pale, sweating, coughing as he lie in a magic-induced sleep.

A harsh breath passed between my lips. "Is he ... getting any better?" I asked, afraid of the answer even before it was given.

"If you're asking if he's healing, the answer is no. Another cursed weapon," she sighed, adding, "But we'll officially have an arsenal of our own to fight back with soon."

At those words, my mood lifted a bit. "Soon?"

She stepped around me, headed for Ivan again as she answered. "Yes, once the Elders finally order their witches to do their jobs. My guess is they'll wait until after tonight's meeting. It will take a considerable amount of magic, so they'd most likely hold off until they're certain their power won't be needed to maintain order during the gathering. You and I both know those things have been known to get out of hand."

Her tone was cold as the sentence trailed off. Maybe she thought it was all too little too late. Maybe she'd grown tired of feeling like the Sovereign was always one step ahead.

Dallas grumbled from across the room. "Well, it's *something*, I guess."

Josiah agreed with a deep grunt.

"The guards have already been supplied with bullets and arrows much like this one," Hilda said flatly, gesturing toward the shaft that had been removed from Ivan's shoulder. "Those who've come to aid in our fight will be directed to distribution stations the Council ordered set up around town, areas not affected by the flood. There will also be extra artillery stashed in designated homes and facilities in the area," she went on.

I took note of how unimpressed she delivered her speech. I was now *positive* she believed the Council had underdelivered.

Her heavy gaze fell on Ivan and stayed there. Hilda wasn't one to let her emotions show through often, but you could almost count on her inability to hide them when it came to one thing.

Family.

Our love for one another was a fault we all shared as a unit. Josiah draped an arm around his aunt's shoulder and she leaned into his side. Seeing Ivan like this was hard. Had there not been so much pressure on us, so much to plan and consider, I was certain most would have fallen apart by now. He was important to us all— a brother, a best friend.

"He'll beat this," Tobias blurted when he stood to approach Hilda from the other direction, placing a hand on her shoulder as she stared down at her nephew's helpless body.

"Well, we have you all to thank for slowing down Sebastian and his men. There isn't much they can do with such a large portion of their supplies missing," she replied.

I could only hope her theory was true.

The others stayed close to Ivan, but my arm was seized by Hilda when she led me aside, wanting to continue our conversation in private.

"They saw it all coming," she whispered.

The somewhat out of place statement jarred me back to the present as I asked for clarity. "They who?"

"The Oracles," she explained. "Two nights ago, when you were away, I was summoned, and they knew everything. Only, I didn't understand how to piece it all together. If I had ..."

Her voice trailed off and that heaviness returned to her expression.

"They tried to warn you?" I asked.

Large, gold earrings quivered when she shook her head and answered.

"No. It doesn't work that way. They're neutral when it comes to the affairs of the existing supernatural world, meaning they're not known to intervene. As ascended beings, they have shed their humanity, no longer sympathizing with our plights except for those instances that concern the supernatural world as a whole. In other words, they aren't exactly concerned with the menial, day-to-day problems we face," she sighed, peering up before continuing. "They have a clearer view of the bigger picture than any of us could ever dream of. So, don't fool yourself for one second. This war is beneath them and most would shed no tears for either side," she said, but then added one last thought. "Except one."

My brow quirked when she uttered those last words.

Her gaze left me and I was nearly holding my breath waiting for her to go on.

"The others rarely do or say things that will change the course of events because they serve a much higher purpose than meddling in our affairs, but there is one who seems to deviate," she shared. "Under his guidance, the others have been known to humor me on occasion. In fact, had it not been for this, bringing Evangeline back would have been impossible. It was their blessing that hid me when circumstances required that I use magic that has long-since been forbidden," she explained, placing her hand on the large, gold pendant that hung around her neck.

"This blessing, these *favors* the Oracles grant you, what's the cost?" I asked. Nothing was ever free.

Hilda shook her head. "No cost. For reasons unknown to me, I simply have favor with the one."

When she finished speaking, I was quiet for a bit. Very rarely did good things just happen; there was always a catch.

"The Oracles, you mentioned they've shed their humanity. Does that mean they once had physical forms?" I asked.

A faint smile lifted the corners of Hilda's mouth. "There are many theories about where the Oracles come from. And while their identities are a mystery, we do know that they seem to circulate, operating on five-thousand-year cycles before being replaced by another high being. With that being said, I cannot say for sure who the ascended soul is that's been so gracious to me, to *us,* but whoever he may be, he does seem to hold some measure of regard for our lives," she shared. "Because of that, when I requested a blessing to assist Elise with the spell that restored Evangeline's soul, he granted it without question. It was unheard of for such a monumental request to be met, but the proof of his kindness toward us is currently walking around on two legs," she added, referring to Evangeline.

There was a distant look of gratitude in her gaze. I was trying to grasp the breadth of what she seemed to be suggesting without suggesting it, but I had to ask.

"Are you implying that this ascended soul, the Oracle who's been assisting you is ... Noah? Evangeline's father?"

Glancing around, Hilda frowned when shushing me. Not that I was loud enough for anyone to hear. "You're putting words in my mouth. I simply said that he, *whoever* he is, seems to have our best interests at heart."

I didn't disagree, but she had definitely said more than that. "So, let's say your theory is correct and the Oracles really *are* ascended souls, former physical beings. Then it'd be possible, right? There's a chance it's him?" I asked quieter this time.

"Anything is possible," she said vaguely. "But it won't do you or anyone else any good to sit around thinking on such things. Elise has found love again in Dallas and I would never burden her with this idea, especially seeing as how it's only that—an idea. So, don't utter a word of this," she insisted, adding, "To *anyone!*"

I understood how speculating could do more harm than good, but the only reason I wouldn't at least mention it to Evangeline was because there was no proof.

"I won't say anything," I assured her. She accepted that, but glared at me long and hard before moving on.

"This last time we communed, they spoke of the child," Hilda revealed. "Their words were indirect and shrouded in vague parables, but I had a pretty good idea of what they meant. Only, my theory wasn't confirmed until Nicholas' episode outside the gate.

The Oracles spoke of a new light returning, and according to them, this light would be powerful, valuable, and ... highly sought after."

My senses became heightened, keener when she uttered those words—*highly sought after*. As in, there would be many who would fight to protect it, and many who'd fight to destroy it. Both fists tightened at my sides.

A fresh wave of rage nearly knocked me to the ground as I considered what that meant, that this child's life could one day soon be at the top of some supernatural hitlist.

"All this because he or she is a descendant of the two originals?"

Hilda was silent for a moment and I could tell she was trying to decide how much to say and how much to hold back. Only, this wasn't the time for filtering.

"Tell me what you know," I demanded, adding, "And even what you *think* you know."

She peered up, her dark, defiant eyes still trying to decide if she'd let me in completely.

"None of what I believe is fact," she said, prefacing the statement to come. "It's all instinct and opinion, but I believe this child will be ... special. If it weren't so, the Liberator would not have been activated. In the past *or* present."

My head lowered, considering all she said. However, when I peered up, she wore a look that suggested she hadn't revealed everything.

"What else is there?" I asked. "What aren't you telling me?"

She continued to hesitate for a moment, but then revealed yet another theory. One I was now certain she only held in to protect me. My heart.

"Liam, I ... I believe the stone Evangeline wore the night she died was more effective than we realize. It's the way the Oracles phrased their revelation that first caused me to wonder." She paused a moment, but then explained herself. "They said a 'new light was returning.' At first, I didn't think anything of it, but then it haunted me. All night," she added. "How on Earth could something new return? Unless ... the soul of the child that died with Evangeline when the Liberator claimed her, entered the stone as well and ... is the same soul that dwells inside her today."

My head spun and I let that sink in, the idea of there being less of a loss than I originally imagined, the idea of being given a complete second chance.

"As I said before, I have no real proof to support this, but ... if you were to ask if I believed this with my whole heart," she said, "I wouldn't hesitate to state that I did."

And now, so did I.

"This all leads me to believe that the child was meant to be quite powerful. So powerful, the spell Maisy cast on Elise centuries ago on Sebastian's behalf evolved to ensure that his or her life be brought to a swift end," she concluded.

Blood boiled in my veins at the thought of it.

"We do not know what greater purpose this child will serve, which is precisely why we need to be certain the Liberator does not succeed again," Hilda went on. "Among those of us in this room, there needs to be an understanding." She paused and came closer, her gaze landing on those still standing in this room.

"What we may all be driven to do will force us to go over the Elders' and High Council's heads if they do not act quickly enough. If it comes to that, the act may cost us our lives, but that child must be protected," she declared. "While I understand we've newly formed an alliance with a few members of the Stokes family, blood is blood," she whispered only to me. "They will always fight for Nicholas' survival, which means they'll turn their backs on us the moment they realize we're not of the same mind. If this child is to live ... Nicholas is on borrowed time."

She held my gaze and said more.

"Believe me, I've tried everything I could think of to change this, including things I have not shared with you or the others, right down to holding Maisy here in Seaton Falls as a prisoner under the Elder's watch."

This news came as a surprise to me, but I suppose it shouldn't have. Turning Maisy loose after using her to complete the restorative spell that brought Elise's sons back would have been negligent.

"I thought I might be able to force her to fix this because she originated the spell," Hilda explained. "But dealing with her only enforced what I already believed—what Nick is cannot be undone. The likelihood of there being a remedy for the darkness within him is slim. Therefore, if one is not discovered by the time Evangeline gives birth," Hilda declared, "Greater measures must be taken."

Her stare stayed trained on me for a long while. It was unlawful to knowingly take the life of a supernatural being without a proper trial and sentencing. I was *also* aware that the wages of such a crime was death, but the thing was, there might not have been time for such formalities. If it came down to Nick or my child, or *anyone* I cared about for that matter, I would always choose family, regardless of alliances.

Hilda spoke again, and when she did, she looked deep within me as she assigned a charge I dutifully accepted.

"The two—your child and the Liberator—cannot coexist," she said firmly. "And where it may become complicated is when it comes to his family, including those you now consider comrades."

My gaze stayed trained on Hilda as she made the circumstances even clearer.

"Losing him at the hands of a member of this household will undoubtedly create a rift, one that can't be mended and could result in retaliation. So, I ask you this: how will you respond when that happens? What are you prepared to do to protect your family?"

My vision, clearer than it had ever been, tinted a deep crimson, shading the edges of the room in red. An unfamiliar sensation filled me from head to toe, a deep-seated ferocity that controlled *me* more than I controlled *it*. I took Hilda's question to heart and answered from the very depths of my soul.

"I'll do whatever it takes."

CHAPTER 8

Nick

I couldn't tell if time was really passing this slowly or if I was losing it. I was certain it hadn't been more than a few hours since I'd seen Richie. He dropped in for a second visit after a meeting a few levels above, in the Elders' chamber. Still, I was pacing the length of my cell like it'd been months.

A caged animal. That's what I was.

My thoughts wandered as I paced, but mostly they lingered on Roz. When we spoke, she shared that something was going on with her. I guessed that, if an Elder and the Chancellor had gone out of their way to visit, it was serious.

She'd experienced a lot of changes lately. Most notably, that she was no longer fully submitted to her father. On several occasions, she'd been able to break the sire bond and act of her own free will. The obvious reason was that she was transitioning, taking on the role as alpha of their small pack of only two. But I wondered if there was more to it, a larger picture I hadn't been able to discuss with her because I was ... *stuck* here. That meant she'd have to face whatever it was without me.

A pang of guilt hit because, through everything, she'd been right beside me. Even when no one else could be.

When no one else *wanted* to be.

Among the many things that had me on edge, a growing concern was that no one had bothered to feed me. I could have complained to Richie about it, but didn't. In a way, I suppose allowing myself to be starved was a means of self-punishment. By now, I should have been weak, seeing as how I'd gone without sustenance for so long, but weak was the exact opposite of what I felt. In fact, I couldn't remember a time I felt stronger.

Which wasn't a good thing.

The magic that had made leaving this place feel like an impossibility didn't exactly feel that way anymore. I noticed it maybe an hour ago, but there was definitely a change. Before, it was like my limbs were weighed down by an invisible force, one I couldn't overpower. Now? I wasn't even completely sure I couldn't pry the bars of my cell apart if I tried hard enough.

At the thought, I eyed them, those wrought-iron posts that separated me from the free world. They kept me from my family, friends ... Roz.

They also kept me from hurting someone else I cared for deeply. Someone who, at the thought of her, I wanted to feel the tendons of her throat in my mouth as I ripped it to shreds.

I crouched and held my head, wishing there was a way to rinse my mind clean of this darkness, but ... there was no remedy. I felt that harsh reality all the way down to my bones. This feeling, this thirst for her death, wouldn't be quenched until the job was done.

Until she no longer breathed.

"Doing all right over there, friend?" came that odd, raspy voice that sent chills down my spine every time I heard it.

She—the only other person I believed to be locked away in this dungeon—had been quiet. I hadn't heard from her since the brief speech she gave when I awoke here, groggy and just coming down from a fit of rage.

Honestly, I was grateful she'd made herself scarce until now. There was something about her strange voice and cryptic messages that made being stuck down here just a little bit creepier. I had to remind myself she couldn't leave her cell any more than I could leave mine. Only then was I able to fall asleep last night. Otherwise, I might have stared past the bars, into the dark, narrow corridor half expecting her to come for me.

I could only guess what she might look like, but you couldn't convince me there wasn't a real-life monster residing in the cell beside mine.

"Ohhhh ... something's happening," she crooned, practically singing the words before a sinister laugh hit the air. "Can you feel it? Can you feel the thinning?" she asked.

The meaning behind nearly everything she said was always vague, open for interpretation. However, tonight, I was positive she spoke of the magic. It was what bound us here and, she was right ... I *could* feel it weakening.

"My guess? The clan's working on something big, something that's pulling on the spell placed on these bars," she explained. With those words, I heard those dry, rough hands of hers slowly caressing the very bars she spoke of.

"If we try, there might be a chance of escaping," she suggested, that same hint of a smile I always sensed mingling within her statement.

I said nothing, just focused on trying to block it all out—her voice, the dark thoughts that continuously rested on the outer fringes of my mind.

"You're a tough one to crack, aren't you?" she commented when I failed to respond. "Don't tell me you're still trying to fight your nature, Nicholas. Still pretending you're not exactly what you are."

A sharp pain in the back of my head brought my lids slamming down, cutting off my line of sight from the bars of my cell. With the stabbing sensation, an image rushed in.

I saw it clear, vivid—a gruesome scene that brought more pleasure than I would ever admit. Walls slathered in blood, a floor covered in more of the same, and in the center of the room ... a body.

Or what was left of one.

Covered in sheer white, blood-stained fabric, Evie lay lifeless, a blank stare fixed on me. Behind that stare, only terror, the last emotion she experienced before death took her.

Before *I* took her.

I squeezed my eyes tight and tried to shake it off, but there was no turning this off. When I opened them again, my gaze landed on my arms. Every vein had gone dark again, filling with the venom that fed the beast.

In her cell, the wicked one laughed—a dark sound I wished I could forget, but knew I never would.

"Just let it in, Nicholas. Just let ... it ... in."

I wasn't sure how, but she knew. Without seeing me, she knew I was losing this fight. Knew there was no contending with what could only be described as the deepest primal urge I believed to exist on the planet.

"Help!"

The desperate plea flew from my mouth without thinking, a final effort to signal someone that things weren't right. If I could just yell loud enough for guards to come down and see the state I was in, see that the thinning magic was no longer enough ... maybe they could stop me.

I was aware that, if this cell could no longer hold me, there was only one other option, but that was better—better than being free and dangerous, better than having to live with the damage I knew I was capable of doing.

"Help!" I called out again, the depth of my voice reverberating off the walls.

"Help me! Please! Pleeeease!" the witch said mockingly, letting out another one of those menacing laughs again right after. "No one's coming, Nicholas," she teased, adding, "It's just you and me."

Another image flickered and, this time, I staggered backwards until my shoulders touched the wall. The scene hadn't changed, but I wasn't satisfied just to see her lying there. I'd begun to feast on Evie's flesh, tearing the softness of it from her bones, feeling the warmth of her slick blood draining down my throat.

I panted, feeling a strange sense of calm fill me as I allowed the fantasy to play out instead of forcing it from my thoughts. I was completely incapable of denying myself such a simple pleasure— the joy of just ... imagining it.

My tense limbs relaxed, breathing slowed. The feeling equated to what I imagined an addict must feel giving in to their vice after years of resisting it.

"That's it," the witch whispered. "Let it in. It's who you are."

No, she was wrong. These thoughts, these *feelings*, weren't natural. They *weren't* who I was. While the urges were purely instinct, I was still aware they were terrible.

Disgusting.

I snapped back to reality with a gasp as my eyes widened. Next, a surge of determination filled me. I was suddenly less content to revel in the idea of succumbing to the darkness. As easy as it would have been—as *satisfying* as it would have been—I had to fight it. The defiance that rocked me to my core caused me to act out of character, doing the one thing I swore I wouldn't.

I engaged.

"It's you," I accused, letting the witch know I was aware she'd taken advantage of the weakening magic to taunt me. "Get out of my head!" I yelled, hearing the forced words rip from my throat.

Her laugh rang out once again, this time seeming to echo off every surface. As if she was ... suddenly everywhere.

Surrounding me.

"Believe me, if I could take credit for the pretty things swirling around inside that mind of yours, I would in a heartbeat. However, whatever you're seeing," she said, "it's only your true self begging to be set free, begging you to stop bridling it."

Fear crept in and inched its way right across my skin. I knew, without a doubt, I'd messed up. Speaking to her, even if only to try shutting her up, was a mistake. Now, regardless of what I said next, she knew she could affect me.

"What would you say if I told you you're, quite possibly, the most perfect being in existence? The embodiment of all that is just and all that is righteous within the supernatural realm?"

I held my head as my body slumped down the wall. I wanted her to stop. She wanted to infect me with her foul thoughts and twisted rationale, but I wouldn't let that happen.

"There's a child, isn't there? A new descendant soon to arrive?" she asked next. "I overheard you speaking of it yesterday."

Each breath I took came unevenly as I tried to recall when I'd mentioned that, when I'd uttered aloud that Evie was expecting. It didn't take long for it to come back to me—the conversation with Roz. I only wanted to fill her in on everything, bring her up to speed on what happened with me, but now ... I realized Roz wasn't the only one I shared this info with.

"Don't you see, Nicholas? You were sent here for a purpose. To restore balance. If it weren't so, my magic would not have seen fit to create you," she explained.

But I didn't want to listen.

So, trying to drown her out, I clamped both hands over my ears now, letting my eyes fall closed again. Meanwhile, the spell continued to deteriorate, meaning I had to fight to ignore that, too. If I didn't, if I focused on how easily I could have broken out, I might have given it a try.

The witch continued to taunt me, but her voice was muffled now. Still, that did nothing to stop the visions she forced—dark and grim as they were. The room around me seemed to vibrate with her energy and I could only hope that, when I opened my eyes again, the spell hadn't broken completely.

"Don't shut me out!"

Her voice came flooding in, piercing the cone of silence I attempted to create around myself. I was convinced she hadn't even said these words aloud, but rather that she'd somehow entered deeper into my thoughts after I all but invited her in by interacting. She, like every other witch, was cunning.

"You're meant to be powerful, revered among the lycans," she insisted.

Her words were practically tangible now as they became harder to drown out.

"Let me help you reach your full potential," she went on. "No one knows you, or what you're capable of, better than I do. After all, you're only who and what you are because of me," she added.

I coiled into myself, shrinking against the wall, putting up the last ounce of fight I had within me to resist her offer.

All around me, that energy that vibrated the very foundation of my cell seemed to explode outward. When my eyes opened, just beyond my line of sight, the sound of metal giving beneath tremendous pressure—twisting and groaning.

I stood and backed away, feeling the pull overpowering me, but I had to resist.

I made up my mind that I wouldn't give in, that I wouldn't allow my nature to rule me. I'd stave off the beast as long as I could, as *hard* as I could.

No one else could make this choice for me. So, deciding that my fate was still in my own hands, I turned to rush toward the back of my cell, but ...

The speech I had just prepared and planned to use to keep myself from going against this new vow was plucked right out of my head. Instead, a *different* sensation had replaced the feeling of determination.

Fear.

She was like nothing I'd ever seen, and the moment I turned to retreat, I was staring directly into her dark, sinister eyes. A small vial of lycan blood hung around her neck, resting on the lapel of a large cloak that stretched the length of her tall frame. Deep crags set in her decaying, leathery skin made her appear more dead than alive. In short, her appearance was nearly as putrid as her smell, and as terrible as I imagined her to be, seeing her in the flesh made it clear my imagination had come up short. Everything about her was frightening and ... indescribable.

I felt confused and lightheaded, trying to grasp how she'd just gotten from her cell and into mine without the door unlatching, but I could only imagine how powerful she was. The twisting metal I heard a moment before had to have been her bars, but she made a show of proving to me that she couldn't be contained, controlled.

A sinister smile donned her expression, revealing blackened teeth. With the look, came a question.

"Will you accept my offer?" she asked. "Are you ready to see who you were meant to be?"

She stared into my eyes and I honestly equated this experience to being face-to-face with evil incarnate. Her demeanor was alarmingly calm as she awaited an answer.

The two sides of me warred—the one wanting to hold on to everything I could to fight for some sense of normalcy, but then there was the other side. The side that constantly pushed me to do the wrong thing.

My voice was hard and unyielding when I finally answered, doing what I could to contain my fears, speaking the only response I felt she deserved.

"Go to hell."

That sick smile of hers grew and I had a hard time reading it, reading *her*. She took a step closer, her foreboding figure cloaked beneath the shroud of the dark robe.

"As you wish," she uttered with a grin, "but do understand; I'll be taking you with me."

Long, bony fingers extended from the sleeve of her robe, clutching a large stone. There was a glint of pleasure in her eyes and there was no doubt she enjoyed the fact that I resisted her. Nearly as much as she enjoyed lifting that stone the next second, wielding it through the air until it struck my skull.

The edges of the room went dim as my body slumped to the stone floor beneath my feet. I was dazed and writhing in pain, but knew it wouldn't be long until everything would go dark. I resisted it as long as I could, because I feared what she'd do to me once I was unconscious, but, eventually, there was no holding it off.

The room around me went black and silent, all except for the sound of a voice whispering the last words I'd hear before going completely under.

"He'll be so happy to see you."

CHAPTER 9

Evie

Heat still lingered from the day, covering my skin even at this late hour. Half my vision fixated on the lush expanse of greenery beyond the terrace, the other half—a smooth, ink-stained back trimmed in moonlight. My hand went there, to Liam's frame and I was starkly aware of not being in our present time.

Even beyond the antiquated setting, I just ... knew.

This was another glimpse of our life before, all set within a dream. I still had no idea how or why this was possible, but it was and I couldn't control it.

My cheek pressed to his back when I moved in closer, letting my eyes drift closed. Beside him I felt safe, protected, like nothing in the world could move me. It wasn't long before, in this vision, I drifted off, recalling the last thought that came before sleep being that of how, the next day, we would venture to the other side of my father's kingdom—our kingdom—to visit a close friend whose face I couldn't recall, but knew by name.

Zahara.

After that ... peace.

It felt like this silence stretched on forever and it reminded me of how I'd visited Liam in the past, wandered into his dreams. Only, this time, I believed I was visiting my own past, wandering into the remnants of my former self's memories.

My eyes opened when a light sound startled me awake, but then ... everything happened so fast. One moment I was peering beyond the pristine, white stone banister that enclosed the terrace. Then, the next ... terror.

I barely had time to make a sound before I was covered by a shadow, a large body with strength like I'd never known before. Within seconds, it had taken me and leapt over the banister, falling several stories to the ground below. Its massive, powerful body absorbed the impact with ease, never slowing as it darted across the property without so much as a glance back.

I managed to peek past the beast's shoulder to catch a glimpse of a flame-covered giant hunting us down.

Liam.

He called out to me and I did my best to shift. But this monster ... it had some how suppressed my ability to change. My dragon struggled to ignite, managed a dim flame that covered my skin, but there was nothing more.

"Evangeline!"

The desperation woven into those four syllables was ... it was heartbreaking. It was the sound of a man chasing down the woman he knew he couldn't live without. I was sure of this because ... I felt the same way about him.

Liam was fast, but this creature that carried me was somehow faster, managing to keep the lead when Liam took flight.

I knew how this would end, because I'd been told this story

before. My heart raced inside my chest as I fought to end the vision, fought to awaken before things went any further. I didn't want to know what it felt like to be ripped limb from limb. Didn't want to be reminded of all that had been taken from me—centuries with the man I love, memories I might never recover.

When I sat up straight in his bed, Liam was startled awake, taking in the sight of me before he spoke—panting, drenched in sweat.

"What is it? What's wrong?" he asked, his panicked tone making it hard to tell whether I was still dreaming or awake.

He sat up beside me, the weight of his arms encircling my shoulders as he brought me close. I couldn't breathe, couldn't speak. The only action my body seemed to comprehend was crying. The tears came hard and fast, choking me up as the details of the nightmare haunted me even now, as I was wrapped in the arms of the one I'd just watched fight to save my life.

It was too much. All of it.

"Something's not right," I finally choked out, feeling the softness of his t-shirt against my cheek as it soaked up my tears. "I can feel it," I explained.

Through the darkness, my eyes searched every corner of the room, carrying the sinking feeling something was coming for me.

"You're safe," he breathed into my ear, kissing the top of my hair the next second. "I have you."

My hands gathered material from his shirt when I squeezed his back, desperately trying to convince myself it had only been a dream, but ... it felt like more than that.

"I was there," I finally whispered, deciding to tell Liam about the visions I'd begun to have.

"You were ... *where?*" he asked, his tone soothing me as I clung to him.

"In the past," I admitted. "*Our* past. The first time, it was the story you told me. The one about how we finally owned our feelings."

Liam was quiet and still as he listened, but I felt his heart beating inside his chest. It picked up speed just a bit, but it was enough to notice.

"We were ... we were in my bedroom," I stammered. "You came to me to apologize, just like you said, but it turned into an argument. Then, before you walked away I asked you that question."

I didn't say anything more, maybe because I was suddenly aware of how insane this sounded, the idea that I had actually gone back to that night and witnessed this. That was impossible. This had to have just been my own interpretation of Liam's rendition of the story. Realizing I'd been irrational, I didn't go on. Instead, I just rested against his chest, reveling in the feel of being held.

"What was the question?"

My ears perked up when Liam asked, fixing my mouth to tell him how silly I'd been to put any kind of stock into these dreams. However, the sincerity in his voice made me think twice. So, I shared.

"I asked you why you cared. Why my actions mattered to you so much."

He was quiet after that. Quiet enough that I felt uncomfortable.

"And what happened next?"

My cheeks warmed with the memory of our conversation moving to the bed and there not being a ton of talking after that. But there was one thing I did recall saying.

"I asked if we should stop because my father might find out," I admitted with a smile, feeling the darkness from tonight's nightmare being burned away.

"And when I offered to stop," Liam cut in, "you were suddenly okay taking the risk."

I didn't say anything, because he was right. Still, I didn't read too much into it because that was vague, a scenario that wasn't so farfetched that fiction couldn't have easily aligned with reality. When I didn't confirm or deny that his response synced with my dream, he asked something else.

"What'd you see tonight?"

That feeling was back, the one that made me awaken in a panic.

"It was ... I saw ... *him*," I said vaguely, not really wanting to relive it—what I saw, what I felt. *Any* of it.

"The Liberator?" Liam asked.

I nodded. "It was the night he came for me."

That stillness in Liam's posture returned and I knew where his thoughts had drifted.

"It was terrible," I shared, pressing my palms against his back. "It was like ... he wasn't even thinking, just acting on pure instinct. And I just had this overwhelming feeling the whole time he carried me that ... it was the end. That he was unstoppable."

That word hung in the air long after I uttered it.

Unstoppable.

It brought back to my memory how Nick had turned on me in the blink of an eye. How he'd seemingly forgotten the bond we shared, a bond that had been the cause of him saving my life once, a bond that had made him come after me when I'd gone to save my parents. We were friends, shared a love for one another that wasn't common. And yet ... it hadn't been enough to stop him from wanting to complete the task.

Killing me.

I didn't realize I was shaking until Liam rubbed my back.

"You're not there," he said reassuringly. "You're here with me. You're safe."

I heard him, but seeing how impossible that thing was to stop, I wasn't sure I believed it.

"Who was Zahara?" The question left my mouth before I could stop myself, but I suppose I just needed to know.

Were the things I was seeing real?

Liam's hand had been moving across my skin in slow circles, but at the mention of her, he stopped.

"I ... I haven't heard that name in years," he said, confirming what I already felt. *She* was real, which meant ... I wasn't losing my mind.

"She was a good friend of yours," he went on to explain. "We had actually made plans to travel to visit her right before you—"

When his sentence ended abruptly, I knew exactly what he was going to say because I had somehow just relived all this in my dreams.

"She and her mate had recently welcomed their first child into the world," Liam explained. "They sent an invitation for us to visit their estate for two weeks, to catch up, to bond with the baby." He paused again before saying more. "She loved you. Deeply. The bond between you two was similar to what you and Beth share. After you passed she ... she never quite recovered from the loss. Last I heard, she and her mate left Bahir Dar and never looked back."

I breathed deep, feeling things I hadn't before. My death had a ripple effect, touching lives beyond those of my family members. I hadn't considered the toll it may have taken on friends, the kingdom as a whole, but now I did. I felt it.

"How can this ... why is this happening?" I asked, feeling the heat of a tear as it streaked down my cheek.

Liam hugged me tighter. "I'm not sure," he breathed. "I didn't even think it was possible."

He'd taken the words right out of my mouth. I, too, thought I'd always feel like my old self and the new were two entirely different beings. However, if these memories continued to puncture the veil, I couldn't help but wonder if my old life was somehow colliding with the present.

"I just wish I knew what it all meant," I admitted aloud.

I had so many questions, so many thoughts to run past Liam, but a frantic knock at the bedroom door made them all scatter.

Liam was on his feet within seconds, snatching the door open to find a wide-eyed Elise standing across the threshold. With so few words, she made the thin sense of security I managed to cling to tonight evaporate into thin air.

"It's Nick," she panted, her gaze shifting to me when adding, "he's escaped."

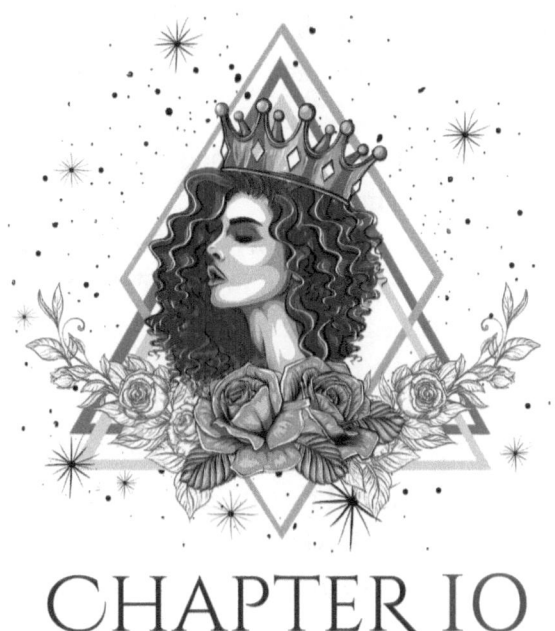

CHAPTER 10

Liam

Five massive wolves darted through the gate, fanning out in all directions as soon as they crossed the barrier. A wall of guards quickly organized just beyond the property line. I should have been out there, scouring the woods with them.

I regretted, now more than ever, having let others steer me from my first thoughts toward Nick ... I should have killed him. So many chances had slipped through my fingers and, for one reason or another, I didn't act. I should have cared less whose feelings would have been hurt, who would have been angry, and just ... did it.

Those whose feelings actually mattered would have gotten over it.

A warm hand touched the back of my arm and I couldn't even look down at her, couldn't look the love of my life in her eyes knowing that beast was out there. Knowing I could have done something about it a long time ago. It felt like I failed ... failed her, failed our child, failed myself.

"Hopefully they'll find him," Evangeline breathed, resting her head against my bicep right after.

"It should have never come down to a *hope*," I seethed, feeling the tension mounting in my limbs, my brow. "I should have done what I knew needed to be done."

Evangeline was silent, but a stern voice from behind filled the void.

"We cannot afford to fall apart right now," Hilda interjected. "Evangeline herself requested that Nick's life be spared on several occasions, so who were any of us to override that decision? It was never *our* lives in danger, only hers. And yet, she saw fit to pardon him."

Hilda's reason only angered me more. None of us could expect Evangeline to choose death for Nick. She was the only one who *hadn't* seen what his kind was capable of. To her, he was more innocent than not because she'd been spared the burden of seeing the Liberator in action. However, after tonight's nightmare, I wasn't sure that was still true, wasn't sure she'd have chosen life for him after experiencing the beast's dark side firsthand.

"If he's out there," Elise chimed in, "my boys will find him."

"And I'll do my part as well," Dallas interjected, jogging down the stairs toward the front door. "Whatever they can't find on the ground, I'll likely find from the air."

Before heading out, he placed a kiss on Elise's cheek and she closed the door behind him.

I wasn't so sure his statement was true, about being able to see more from above than the guys could see from the ground. In my rage, I spoke my thoughts aloud.

"That might have been true if Nick wasn't out there with Maisy," I pointed out.

Having one of the most wicked, most powerful witches in the world on your side would definitely make things more difficult for anyone trying to come for you.

This scenario was the perfect storm. Nick had motive, means, and now a secret weapon who owed us one for capturing her and forcing her to do a spell against her will. I couldn't have put together a more perfect worse-case scenario if I tried.

"We can't lose heart," Elise sighed, reiterating Hilda's thought, but I couldn't listen anymore. "Based on what the Elders have told me, it appeared to have been Maisy who broke out of her cell—bars pried apart, mangled. Nick's lock had been broken and there was blood on the floor, as if there'd been a struggle. For all we know, this is all on Maisy and he was taken against his will. The Elders' witches had a large task to perform tonight and it could have weakened many spells they cast, including that which sealed the cells. Maybe they—"

"And yet, no one thought of that when it actually mattered, when something could have been done to prevent it," I cut in, shortening Elise's explanation because I didn't want to hear it.

Too little too late.

The bottom line was, Nick was out. The logistics were of little consequence at this point.

"We'll be in the basement until we get the all clear," I grumbled. "My best defense is to hide her behind the false wall. I'll stand guard outside it and pray I'm able to take him down before he finds a way beyond it."

That was it. The best I could do was hope that putting my own life on the line was enough to save hers.

I managed to take two steps toward my destination before Hilda's voice rang out again.

"Liam, wait."

My name being called halted me.

"I've got something to say and it cannot be put off," she declared.

When I turned to face her, her expression was grim—the first sign things were about to get even darker. We couldn't take any more bad news and, judging by what I saw, that's exactly what this was.

More bad news.

More of the same.

"I know the timing of what I need to share is, perhaps, the worst it could possibly be, but this is all out of my control," she began. "Liam, after our conversation yesterday, after seeing the materials Sebastian has been stockpiling, I conducted a bit of research. That research included reaching out to several close friends whom I trust—in terms of loyalty *and* knowledge," she assured us, keeping her gaze trained on me. "I explained to you that one possibility for Sebastian's intentions with such a large quantity of biremede stone *might* be to commune with the Oracles. However, you'll also remember I stated that he may have *other* uses for the stones. Uses that were not quite as apparent."

My fists clenched at my sides and I didn't bother breathing, knowing whatever she'd say next would only steal it away.

"What sorts of other uses?" Elise asked, concern clearly marking her expression.

Hilda sighed and moved into the center of the foyer where we had all convened.

"To fully explain, you need to understand a few things that aren't common knowledge," she began. "As you all know, I'm able to commune with the Oracles, which is not typically heard of for a witch. They interact with Elders and members of the High Council, but ... never other supernatural beings. After I boldly petitioned them for help years ago, fully expecting to be rejected, I was granted special permissions for reasons I am not entirely certain of," she shared, passing a glance my way.

I assumed these special permissions she spoke of being granted had something to do with another theory she revealed the day before. She hinted toward a belief that one of the Oracles might possibly be the ascended soul of Noah.

Her brother.

"Being able to commune with the Oracles is all part of a bigger process. There are rules," she explained. "Rights. Responsibilities. One such responsibility is carried out every twenty-ninth or thirtieth day, at the top of the synodic month when the moon is full. It is an event of sorts known as The Syphoning."

We were all silent as she opened our eyes to aspects of the supernatural world that had never been spoken of in our presence. Mostly, because these *events* generally only occurred with Elders, who were notoriously secretive when it came to the ways of the lycans.

"These events consist of the Oracles drawing information from Elders and the knowledge is relinquished involuntarily during a deep, trancelike sleep. It is the same all over the world. At the stroke of midnight on that day, every Elder of every clan participates. It has always been this way. Think of it as a similar process to downloading information. Only the transfer is between the Oracles and the clan leaders."

This was all so foreign to us, difficult to grasp. So, seeing our collective confused expressions, she explained further.

"Because of my connection, I undergo this syphoning event as well. Meaning, whatever information I have, the Oracles are privy to it as well. It is my belief that Sebastian has been using the stones as a conduit of sorts since he arrived in this state, a means of intercepting information from the Elders within a certain radius as they commune with the Oracles, essentially granting himself access to the same information the Oracles have. Like a virus, infecting the entire system."

"So, if this only happens once a month, that means he knows

nothing that's been discussed and planned since the last full moon, right?" Elise asked. There was no missing the hint of panic thinly hidden beneath the words.

Hilda's grim expression answered the question long before she even spoke.

"I believe Sebastian—impatient as he's known to be—is no longer content to wait for monthly updates. Based on the sheer quantity of biremede, some of the other materials you reported finding ... I have reason to believe he's discovered a way to mimic and recreate these events, a way to read those of us marked for syphoning within a given radius ... including myself."

My heart sank. The pieces all began to fit together at once. It now made sense why Sebastian was always two steps ahead, why we assumed there was a traitor among us. No one had leaked information.

It had been stolen.

It was now clear how he knew the clan's plan to fake a weakness in the dam, beating us to the punch by creating a *real* emergency. It was now clear how he knew exactly what Nick was and that the presence of death seemed to fuel his dark side. With this knowledge, we could assume that anything *we* were aware of ... he would be, too.

There was a hush in the room as I believe we all tried to take in the breadth of what had just been revealed. If Hilda was right about this, when Sebastian succeeded, we would have absolutely no secrets.

A brief flicker of emotion behind Hilda's eyes was snatched away when she lifted her head again.

"It is because of this, that I must leave."

The statement drew the air from the room.

"My presence here has become a liability and I cannot justify putting all of you in further danger," she expressed. "If Sebastian has not already weaseled his way inside my head, it will not be long until he does. And if that happens, all our plans, every action we strategize to take against him in the future ... he'll see it coming."

I was right to believe this news was terrible. Having a powerful witch on our side was perhaps our strongest line of defense. But now, it seemed that having Hilda here had suddenly become our greatest weakness.

"I'll be gone within the hour," she announced, shocking us all with this abrupt timeline. "Prolonging my exit will only jeopardize your position even more," she added.

Her eyes glistened and I was aware of what a difficult thing this was for her. She'd sacrificed so much to be here, to make sure we were all safe, at times putting her *own* safety on the line. We wouldn't have gotten this far without her. Her love wasn't shown through soft words or affection, but rather by her loyalty.

I could relate to that completely.

This decision was noble and I respected that she didn't keep this information to herself. No matter how difficult it would be to leave us.

"Where will you go?" Elise asked, doing her best not to sound frantic. "Will Sebastian be looking for you?" she added.

Hilda shook her head. "He'll have no reason to. I'm not the one he's after."

That declaration was sobering because we all knew exactly who among us Sebastian *was* after.

"And because Ivan is under my care, I'm sure you'll agree it's best if he comes with me. I can continue to look after him and keep him out of harm's way while you all find a way to bring me the witch that did this to him. Until then, this is no place for someone in his condition," she added.

Elise gave a nod, but said nothing while keeping her eyes trained on her oldest friend, her sister by marriage.

Evangeline stepped forward, releasing my hand to go to her

aunt's side. A long gaze passed between them. These two, in both lifetimes, had been so much alike. Yes, Hilda was a bit brash and hard to read, while Evangeline was all heart, but ... their strength, their loyalty ... it was unmatched, only rivaled by Elise's.

Evangeline didn't hesitate to bring Hilda into a tight embrace, one that was swiftly returned.

"I won't be here in the flesh, but just know I'm doing everything I can to keep you safe from a distance," Hilda said as they clung to one another. "He will not win again," she added.

Evangeline nodded against her shoulder as the whites of her eyes tinted red, pooling with tears. Hilda stood back, placed a kiss on the forehead of her only niece, and then quickly ascended the steps to gather her things.

Evie

Nick was gone without a trace.

My brothers had returned from their search and came up with nothing. It was Declan who stated he couldn't even catch a *hint* of Nick's scent. Maisy's smell either, which seemed impossible, considering the odor she carried with her the night Elise had her captured and brought to us.

Discovering that there was no lead to point us toward where Nick had gone was just another blow. We were all bewildered, beaten down by one bad circumstance after another. Add to that list that Hilda had just dropped the mother of all bombs on us—the announcement that she'd be leaving.

The guys returned to this terrible news, finding out that our aunt would have to leave us tonight. We depended on her in ways I couldn't even begin to express, but in short, the lack of her presence would definitely be felt.

I understood the reason she had to leave, though, and the decision was made for all the right reasons.

Because, above all else, she wanted to protect us.

"I've got the essentials," Hilda announced as she descended from the second floor. With a small bag tossed over her shoulder, Dallas followed behind her with two larger ones.

The length of her teal skirt dragged the floor in the back where a short train followed. Her style, like her personality, was so bold—something I'd definitely notice was missing from our home once she was gone. Granted, she had put me in my place on more than one occasion, but she'd always only ever done so in love.

An emotion I knew she felt reciprocated from each one of us.

"Are you sure there isn't another way?" Elise asked, stepping forward as Dallas exited with the luggage.

Hilda shook her head and it wasn't lost on me that this was just as hard on her as it would be on the rest of us. Maybe even more so because it was such an abrupt change. The moment she realized the potential danger, she knew what needed to be done.

She *always* knew what needed to be done—something else to miss about her. I could only hope we would get along okay in her absence.

She stood in the doorway and it was abundantly clear she was reluctant to part ways. The feeling was mutual for all parties.

"You'll return the moment things settle," Elise insisted, doing all she could to mask the wetness that pooled in her eyes.

Hilda gave a nod. "As quickly as I'm able to make it here," she assured us. "In the meantime, don't worry about Ivan. He'll be well taken care of. Where we're going, we'll be among other witches, among friends, and I assure you he'll be my main priority."

Ethan was the first to rush in with a hug, and the rest of us followed, swarming Hilda as we swallowed the bitter pill we'd been dealt tonight.

"Don't make a fuss," she insisted when we released her. Swiping a tear from beneath her eye, she corrected her posture and it wasn't long before she appeared as poised and collected as usual.

"I need to get Ivan settled, so I'd better be on my way. And when Dallas returns from the drop point, you'd be wise not to ask questions. The fewer people with knowledge of where I am, the better our chances of *Sebastian* not knowing. Thus, making it nearly impossible to hunt me down for intel should he get desperate."

Elise and Liam agreed.

"Duly noted," Declan replied.

There was a long stint of silence and the heaviness of the moment could be sensed.

Felt.

"Well ... until we meet again," Hilda said in parting, breaking all our hearts the next instant when she stepped outside, closed the door ... and left us.

It was quiet. Eerily so as we all stared at the spot she occupied only a moment ago. It was hard to imagine how we would move forward without her, but we would have to find a way.

"We have to call a meeting," Elise announced, swiping rogue tears from beneath her eyes as she worked to hold her expression.

"With whom?" Dallas asked, following her with his gaze as she began to pace the length of the foyer.

"The entire clan," she declared. "Losing Hilda is a tragedy. Let us not have it be in vain by not doing what we can to plug this information leak. The people need to understand why Sebastian has been on to our every move. They need to know that, while no, the Elders are not untrustworthy, they must now be left out of all our tactical planning and cannot be *told* they're being left out. We have to operate in total secrecy," she declared, our latest loss no doubt driving this sudden staunch focus.

"She's right," Liam interjected. "We'll arrange it tonight."

Elise nodded. "With the Elders and Council only acting as a false headship from this point forward, we'll need to establish new leaders among us. That can be decided at the rally, but we need to decide who will speak, who will pass along what we know."

My stomach rolled with fear, but I imagined it would *always* be that way. I would always feel like I was inadequate to fill the role I was destined to fill. However, that was no longer a sufficient excuse. Fear was not a good enough reason to hide when our people needed hope, needed direction.

"I'll do it," I volunteered.

Every single eye turned my way, but I didn't let that intimidate me. Instead, I stepped forward, coming from behind Liam where I'd chosen to stand when this conversation began. Now, front and center, I fought the urge to shrink into the shadows again, but instead of giving in, I clasped my hands together.

You're queen.

You're queen.

I repeated this to myself like a mantra and, surprisingly enough, each time the words left my mouth, I believed it a little more.

"Most of them don't even know my face," I began. "If I passed them on the street, I could blend in and no one would even think twice. But ... maybe it's time I step up. Time I stop fighting who and what I really am." I glanced around at my family and said more. "I want to be the queen they deserve. I can't do that if I'm afraid to even acknowledge it."

Whereas, I had started out hoping for input as to whether the others thought this was a good idea or not, I had decided all on my own.

"I'll address them tomorrow night. I'm ready. They're ready."

The expressions around the room were a mashup, but I didn't

focus on them. My ability to lead could not be contingent on who did or didn't believe in me—family or not. It had to come from within. And while, on the outside, I hadn't quite found the confidence required to do the job, I had certainly found it on the inside.

My time to lead was here and now ... and no one could take that away from me.

CHAPTER II

Nick

Chipped paint and barred windows—my new surroundings.

The smell of standing water and filth nearly overpowered every other scent I detected. All except the mix of lycans and witches. I felt them all around, like a million eyes set on me from every direction despite not being able to focus on any of the looming figures I caught glimpses of.

I blinked, but things weren't any clearer. I had no choice but to lie there, waiting for my senses to align.

"I implore you, Your Highness. Please consider this beautiful creature before you a peace offering."

I still didn't have a visual, but I knew that voice well. It was the witch from the cell beside mine. The one who'd taken a stone to my head and dragged me God-knows-where for a purpose I hadn't completely figured out yet. All I knew was she seemed to hope someone considered me valuable enough to use as a bargaining chip.

Hard-soled shoes echoed against the cement floor, coming closer. I made out a dark frame—tall and wiry. The figure stooped beside me, crouching only a foot or so away, and it was then that the fog cleared.

The Sovereign, with Blaise following close behind.

Both knew the moment I became aware, prompting two wide grins to part their thin lips.

"Pleasure to see you again, friend," Sebastian groaned.

I hurried to sit upright, thinking I'd get to my feet the next instant, but ... no, that didn't happen.

I yelled out in pain, feeling the burn of what could only be described as a searing-hot knife burrowing deep inside my skull. I fell to my knees again, clinging to the floor.

"There, there," Sebastian said, his calm tone contrasting my own pain. "We can't have you running wild now, can we? Just to be on the safe side, I've had my witches make certain you mind your manners during your stay."

He paused a moment, staring down on me like some sort of science exhibit, and then addressed his son. "Do you think he enjoyed our gift?"

The hairs on the back of my neck stood on end as I realized what *gift* he spoke of—the bodies, hundreds he'd murdered just to taunt me.

"I'd say it did the trick," Blaise agreed, nonchalantly polishing a long, curved blade from where he leaned against a wall. "Looks like it brought the beast right out of him. Just like you said it would," he concluded.

Maniacal bastard ...

I had Sebastian's attention again. "Now we only need to send out a team to confirm he's done what he was born to do. If we're lucky, he took care of our little problem and Elise is mourning her daughter as we speak … all one-thousand pieces of her," he added with a twisted laugh.

His description filled my thoughts with vivid imagery and I fought to suppress it.

I needed to get my bearings so, first chance I got, I could run. Glancing around, I took in my surroundings, hoping to see something familiar, some indicator that I was still in Seaton Falls and only needed to find my way to an exit.

"Pardon me, Your Highness," Maisy spoke up.

Before she could finish, Sebastian turned his head slowly as the corners of his mouth curved downward, giving way to a look of disgust when his eyes landed on her. In response, the witch lowered her gaze to the floor.

"What … is it, Maisy?" Sebastian spat, doing nothing to hide that her interruption was an unwelcomed one.

"I just wanted to point out that, while death and carnage certainly helped his process along, what tipped the boy over the edge was something far more interesting. Something I'm certain you'll be eager to hear, especially seeing as how the other royals hoped to keep it secret," she groveled.

My heart raced knowing what the witch, Maisy, intended to do. The secret she spoke of, the one she discovered by eavesdropping my conversation with Roz, could *not* be shared. Especially not with *this* tyrant.

"Stop," I choked out, barely able to speak with the hold Sebastian's coven had on me. My plea was so weak, it went ignored.

Sebastian took slow steps in the opposite direction as the click of his soles and metal-tipped walking stick created an offbeat rhythm. He stopped with no more than a foot of space between him and Maisy. He was calm, his posture stiff, which made the sudden movement that came next even more jarring.

His thin fingers seized Maisy's throat. If I hadn't known his strength already, I would have now with how easily he lifted her from the ground. He held her there, dangling in the air expressionless as he spoke, unmoved by her nails tearing at the flesh of his hand as she fought to get free.

"Let me be abundantly clear on a few points," he seethed, speaking the words through clenched teeth. "There *are* no other royals. There is but one Sovereign," he declared as Maisy sputtered. "And secondly, there are no secrets among the Seaton Falls clan. I've made certain of that," he added. "So spare me your lies."

When he finished speaking, he dropped Maisy to the floor in a heap. She gasped, sputtering for air. Meanwhile, Sebastian pulled a black handkerchief from his lapel pocket to wipe his hands clean of her filth. Giving Maisy his back, he addressed Blaise.

"She's of no use to me. Have her taken out back and executed."

"Please, Your Highness!" Maisy begged. "After what I've done here today, bringing you such a special creature … please, have mercy."

Silence filled the room and my stare was trained on Sebastian. For a moment, he ignored Maisy's plea, but with a look of amusement set on his face, he turned and asked a question.

"Now, why … on Earth … would I do a silly thing like that?"

Maisy's expression went blank and she had no response.

Sebastian paced while speaking. "From the moment I realized what Nicholas was, he was destined to end up right where he is now—in my possession, soon to be mine to control at will. With his help, Seaton Falls will be all but wiped off the map. And with that single act, the rest of the clans will fall in line once again and order will be restored."

He laid eyes on Maisy again, adding more.

"You did nothing here today but save my men a trip to Seaton Falls. The Liberator would have been retrieved without your … *help*," he concluded, reminding the witch of her place in this world. "Now, if you'll excuse me, there's work to be done."

"You're mistaken," Maisy called out when Sebastian had just begun to walk away.

From the sound of his heavy sigh, it was apparent he was over Maisy speaking out of turn. However, when she stood again, I guessed she didn't care. I imagined staring death in the eye could have that effect, make someone bold when they otherwise ought not to be.

Without waiting for his father's command, Blaise stepped forward, seizing Maisy by the arm. It took him and three other soldiers to move her even the few feet they managed, but when she spoke again, it was Sebastian who halted them.

"She's not dead!" Maisy yelled out. "You mentioned Elise mourning her daughter's death, but that's not so," she shared. "One might even guess Elise has cause to celebrate."

I fought harder now, hoping I could stop Maisy from saying another word. If I couldn't, if I failed ...

"Evangeline is with child," Maisy blurted, causing my heart to sink. "She and the dragon known as Reaper."

My eyes slammed shut and I acknowledged the strange mix of emotions within me. The dark side that wished Evie dead, the *real* me who wanted nothing more than to protect her. As hard as it was to explain, it was ten times harder to understand.

"What did you just say?"

With Sebastian's question, and the clear return of an inkling of leverage, Maisy shrugged away from Blaise and the soldiers.

"You heard correctly, Your Highness," she reiterated. "And it was *this* event that awakened the Liberator. It appears he thirsts *not* for the blood of the hybrid, but ... for the one that grows within her."

My stomach turned when she finished that statement, suggesting that ... the one I was after was ... the child?

That couldn't have been.

Not even a monster would want that.

Maisy had clearly piqued Sebastian's interest this time, and his anger. I couldn't tell what fueled it exactly, but I guessed it was either that I'd left the job undone, or that whatever intel he *thought* he had wasn't as accurate as he believed it to be.

"A child," Sebastian said to himself, his thoughts drifting as he paced, nearing a window that had been blacked out with dark paint. "Hm."

"It would be a glorious feat for the kingdom if the child were to be seized and sired, Your Highness. Once the family has been done away with, nothing would stand in your way from yielding the little one to serve only you—a powerful hybrid to obey and do your bidding, to revere *you* as his or her father."

"Silence, Maisy," Sebastian hissed, shutting her up immediately. He turned to Blaise to speak. "This changes everything."

Blaise nodded, agreeing, but next his gaze was set on me. "If she's right about this thing thirsting for the kid's blood, that could present a slight conflict of interest. It might be impossible to keep both in our possession without *this* one trying to take bites out of our hybrid."

I was disgusted hearing them speak of two lives so callously, as if they wagered a business deal.

"You bring up a good point," Sebastian replied, distracted as he thought.

"Unless, Maisy being the one who created him, can somehow fix him? Make it so he and the child could co-exist?" Blaise suggested.

The idea made Sebastian turn toward Maisy. "Can it be done?"

My eyes flitted to her, too, wondering if ... maybe ...

However, her expression turned dim right before answering. "His existence is bound by my magic. What's done is done," she concluded, admitting she had no more control over me than I had over myself.

Sebastian was clearly disheartened by this information when he sighed. "Very well then." With a quick look exchanged between him and Blaise, he gave clear instructions. "I suppose we have ourselves a hybrid to capture," he sighed. "But first, begin the siring process. The quicker we get the Liberator started on my blood, the sooner we can put him to work."

"And what about the witch?" a soldier called out.

Sebastian cast an indifferent glance toward Maisy before sealing her fate. "She's just said herself that she's useless to us. Kill her and make it quick."

"No, please. You're Highness, I ... No!"

She was hauled beyond the thick cinderblock walls, and her screams seeped right through them. I could only guess how Maisy met her end, but the moment of her death was marked by eerie silence.

She'd brought me here today, hoping for Sebastian's favor, but all she'd done was get herself killed moving me from one prison to another. Only, as ten soldiers inched toward me with menacing grins on their faces—one carrying a bucket of thick, red liquid and a short hose—I was positive Maisy had kept her word.

She promised she'd drag me right to hell with her ... and this was certainly that.

Hell.

CHAPTER 12

Evie

"Sure you're ready for this? Ready to be the center of attention," Beth clarified.

I lifted my gaze toward where she sat on the end of my bed, giving the only answer I had. "Doesn't matter if I'm ready. We're out of time."

She rushed over as soon as she got my call—unloading all my problems on her, because, well ... that's what best friends are for.

My condition was, technically, supposed to stay within the family, but she was exactly that to me. She knew all my secrets— how I lost myself when Liam was down, how I nearly self-destructed, and she had my back through it all. It didn't feel right keeping the biggest news of my life from her, nor did I see the point in hiding that, tonight, during the rally Liam spread the word about, I would finally step out from the shadows. It was time the people knew I was ready for this.

Born for this.

As the sun sank below the treetops just outside the window, Beth was seated across from me. I leaned against the headboard, thinking of how weird it felt being in this room. I hardly came in here anymore, into this space Elise had so carefully furnished with me in mind. Most of the things I used on the daily had migrated to Liam's dresser, his drawers, his closet. The transition was gradual. I hadn't made a huge gesture by deciding to haul my things in all at once, but with each day, the line between what was his and mine blurred even more.

However, this room served its purpose in times like these, when a girl needed to talk to her best friend in private.

"I'm so sorry about your brother," Beth said.

Taking a deep breath, I nodded before replying. "It's so strange. I hardly know the six of them, but there's such a deep connection and love I feel already. I think that might be because my dragon hasn't forgotten *anything*. She's holding on to my brothers, Elise, Hilda, just like she held on to Liam."

Beth reached out and my hand warmed in hers when she held it. She seemed to understand despite it sounding a bit odd.

"And ... I've been having the strangest dreams the past couple nights," I admitted. "At least, I thought they were dreams, but ... the more I think about it, the more I'm sure they're *not*."

I glanced up just as her brow quirked. "What do you mean?"

An answer didn't come right away. Mostly because I had no idea how to explain, but I tried.

"I think they're ... memories. *My* memories. After talking to Liam about them, too many facts line up for it not to be real," I shared. "It was weird. Liam was present in both, but we weren't in *this* time. Everything—the entire setting, our clothes, the way we spoke—it was all from before. Like ... *long* before," I added with another smile. "He once told me about the moment I finally stopped denying my feelings for him. In the vision, there were definitely traces of what he shared with me, but … more. More detail, more emotion."

I could have told her about the dark nightmare from the night before, but it was still too haunting.

Beth moved her thick, blonde hair behind her shoulder before responding. "It's probably the baby."

I laughed a bit. "You think?"

She nodded while explaining. "I've heard of women having strange dreams when they're expecting, so … it's possible. And because you're a supernatural being, this experience is kinda supernatural, too. Instead of dreaming you're giving birth to an alien or something crazy like that, he or she's helping you see your past."

If I'd learned anything since I first started sensing Liam, it was that dreams of him were rarely simple. Keeping that in mind, this theory of hers could have been true.

"One thing's for sure," I sighed. "You're dead on about this experience leaning toward being anything *but* normal."

"Of *course* it's not normal," she scoffed. "I mean, you've had the entire *world* thrown at you these past few days. I'd say a minor freak out is allowed."

It was nice to be understood. Not that everyone else didn't get me, but that understanding was different coming from another girl, one my age. Beth could easily put herself in my shoes and relate to how all these changes might make an eighteen-year-old feel kind of overwhelmed. And another thing I knew she'd relate to was my concern for a mutual friend, despite him having tried to kill me a couple days ago.

"So, have you heard anything new?" I asked, drawing my legs closer when I clarified. "About Nick, I mean."

Beth's expression turned somber when she shook her head. "Only that his family's gone looking for him. You?"

I sighed before speaking. "Nothing but the fact that there were signs of a struggle in his cell, which means he was likely taken against his will."

We were quiet, maybe both worrying if he was safe, or even alive. Maybe both worrying if *I* was safe with him roaming around out there. But with time winding down, I didn't want to talk about that. If I was going to have my head in the game for this rally, I couldn't focus on him.

On being *afraid* of him.

"Your parents tell you stuff," I blurted, changing the subject. "Any chance you heard of something called cresting?"

When one eyebrow lifted, I took that as a no, and then sighed when she answered. "Not that I can recall. Why? Should I have?"

I shook my head. "No, but I thought ... maybe there was a chance you'd read about it and could help me figure something out."

Her foot bounced over the edge of my bed when she asked, "Figure *what* out?"

The short answer to a really long explanation was, "I was hoping you might know of a way to tell how I would *'present'* as Elise put it. Apparently, because I'm a hybrid, this pregnancy could go either way."

That word ... pregnancy ... it felt strange rolling off my tongue. I did my best to hide the fact that I didn't think such a term would apply to me before age twenty-five or thirty.

"Dumb this down for me," Beth laughed.

"Lycans carry a kid for nine months like a human. Dragons? Try three," I revealed, watching as her expression shifted from bearing a huge grin to going slack in a matter of seconds.

"My sentiments exactly," I added. "And ... I guess I'll have my answer in a couple weeks."

"Holy stretchmarks, Batgirl. Are you freaking kidding me?"

Leave it to her to make me laugh when I was honestly about to freak out again.

"Nope. Definitely not kidding."

There was a strange silence I didn't expect. Beth was never short on words. Never. During that stretch of time, her eyes stayed trained on my face and there weren't many people who could read me better than she or Liam could. And I knew that was exactly what she was doing.

"I, for one, don't think that's the end of the world. My mom always tells me that being thrown a curveball just gives you an opportunity to get creative. So, let's get creative," she said with far more pep than I was capable of mustering at the moment.

"Tell me your biggest worry with all this," she demanded as she continued to stare.

There were *several* worries, but she asked about the biggest, so that's what I shared.

"That they'll all be so worried about *me* they won't take care of themselves."

When I finished speaking, Beth nodded slowly.

"You know how Liam is," I explained. "He'll put everything he has into protecting me, forsaking even himself if he has to."

Beth's expression turned thoughtful.

"Have you ... considered going someplace safe?" she asked.

I nearly rolled my eyes, having heard this speech too many times to count.

"It's been brought up once or twice," I said sarcastically. "But to answer your question, no, I'm not considering it."

I didn't bother going into the many reasons that wasn't feasible. Including that I knew it wouldn't actually keep me *or* them any safer.

"And ... at the risk of being a Debbie-Downer ... you're sure speaking tonight is a good idea?" she asked.

While I knew tonight would take a ton of courage, I was honestly surprised Beth wasn't more on board. I must have said as much through my expression because she rushed to clarify right after.

"I don't mean to scare you or anything," she explained. "It's just that ... maybe staying in the background for a little while longer isn't such a bad idea."

I studied her for a moment, detecting that there was more lurking beneath the surface, and then when wetness touched her eyes, I was *sure* of it. I moved from my seat at the headboard to sit beside her.

"What is it?" I asked, squeezing her hand again.

Beth's gaze met mine and she didn't bother trying to hide her tears.

"I just ... I can understand your family wanting to do everything they can to protect you. I—"

When her voice trailed off, my heart raced, wondering what she'd say next. She was the toughest girl I knew, so for her to be fighting tears right now meant whatever she was holding was major to her.

She swiped her finger beneath her eye and sniffled. "Sorry for crying. This is so stupid," she added, laughing at herself. "It's just that, I've been thinking very hard about sending my parents away."

My brow twitched at her wording. "Send them away? What do you mean?"

She moved more tears from her cheek and sat up from her comfy position, explaining a bit. "You've had a lot going on, so I didn't want to bother you with this, but ... the transition is complete. You're officially sitting in the presence of a true-blue alpha female."

There should have been pride laced within that statement, but instead, only sadness. When she spoke again, I understood why.

"My parents want to run. Want our entire family to run," she clarified. "And honestly, being able to feel how weak they are now in comparison to me? I want nothing more than to do

130

just that," she admitted. "But not for me, to save *them*. To spare them from what's coming." She seemed embarrassed to share what she said next. "Out of fear, I even forbid them from coming tonight."

With the lycan race being so proud, I was certain Beth wouldn't have said such things in anyone else's presence, but I was glad she knew she could share with me.

"I *can't* turn my back on the clan, but ... Evie, all I keep thinking is that I can't lose my parents. I can't let them ... I—"

She couldn't even finish the statement. However, I understood completely. I couldn't imagine what it must have felt like to foresee the likelihood of your parents being killed, all the while possessing the power to command that they flee to safety. There was undoubtedly a pull within her to respect their wishes and flee, but also feeling inclined to honor the clan.

As a girl who'd lost her parents—albeit in a different sense than what Beth feared—I would have given *anything* to change that.

"I can't leave," she repeated. "It's not in me to run when I know what's coming, My friends and family are the most important thing in the world to me and there are too many that I care about in this town to turn my back. And with you carrying the future of *both* shifter races ... I need to be here."

I didn't know what to say. Her loyalty was something to marvel at. She and I were alike in that way—hence the reason I was still dwelling under this roof despite being given a means of escape.

I sat straight, considering my words before uttering them. "Well, I can't tell you what's best for you or your parents, but ... what I *can* tell you is that I support your decision either way. And if you do decide to send them off, you're more than welcome to stay with us."

She seemed a little lighter when I made the offer. "I'd like that."

"Well, as a fair warning, things can get kind of chaotic around here with there being so many of us, but … I'd be happy to have you. We *all* would," I amended.

Beth laughed and my gaze was trained on her, this brave girl who'd shown me so much about myself, about what true friendship was. She'd been with me through everything and … I don't know … that was kind of priceless.

"I guess I have some things to consider. I'll sit down and talk to them after the rally," she concluded.

I nodded, still holding her hand. "I think that's a good idea."

Deep in thought, she sniffled a bit and I figured we ought to talk about something else.

"So … what's it like being the alpha female?" I asked with a smile.

She returned the gesture. "Pretty cool, but probably pales in comparison to being queen."

I nudged her shoulder when I laughed. "Do you feel any different? Has to be wild being able to boss your entire family around with a simple glare, right?"

"Well … not the *entire* family."

Unsure of what she meant, I passed her a questioning look that prompted her to explain, and she did with just one name.

"Roz."

I didn't know much about her other than that she was with Nick now and she and Beth didn't get along. So, to say it came as a surprise that the slight-built brunette was *also* an alpha was a bit of an understatement.

"Wow … two alpha females in one family. That's kinda wild."

"Actually, one *pack* alpha, and one *clan* alpha. Officer Chadwick shifted down and Roz is officially being groomed to lead the clan, ranking just below the Elders. There hasn't been an official announcement—mostly because the Elders are concerned the clan will freak out that their fate kinda lies in the hands of children—no offense," she said before pausing. "But as soon as everything dies down, they'll get the word out. They've been working with her in secret."

Again, I was speechless.

"But at least now I understand why I've always lightweight hated her," Beth added, baring a half smile before explaining. "Apparently, it's a thing between pack alphas and clan alphas. Part of me, something within my wolf, has always felt the pull of her authority and sort of resisted it. It's like ... ego times a million," she joked after figuring out how to put the feeling to words.

"And now?" I asked. "Does it *still* feel that way between you two? Is it better? Worse?"

She shrugged. "Better. Even if only marginally. But my mom says it subsides with time, so ... maybe I won't always want to heave the poor girl over a cliff."

Being soft wasn't Beth's gift, but she was loveable nonetheless.

"Well, I guess if things can work out between the two of *you,* this little bit of business with the Sovereign should be a piece of cake, right?" I said with a weary smile.

Humoring me, Beth smiled back. "Yup ... simple as pie."

Now, if only I actually believed that.

CHAPTER 13

Liam

Everyone showed up. And I do mean everyone.

The only members of the clan missing were the Stokes family, including Roz, Chris and Lucas who'd joined the hunt for Nick. The Elders were, of course, also not in attendance, which had been by design. It was crucial that we got our message across to the entire body of lycans here in Seaton Falls, but equally crucial that no member of the High Council be aware of our gathering.

The flames of tall torches carved out a path among the trees. They were all that illuminated the space. Our family stood at the center of a circle, one composed of twenty large, Kevlar chests, each stocked with the weapons the witches had laced with magic. In preparation for tonight, several of us had gone to the artillery stations where they'd been stored, scattered about the woods, and brought them here. This rally seemed like the perfect time to arm the people, give them a sense of security. Until now, they'd only been given the Council's word. Tonight, they'd be given more. They'd be given weapons, something *tangible* to ensure their safety.

Despite the massive crowd, it was eerily quiet, much like the chamber before a Council meeting commenced. I suppose that was an indication that *this* event was being treated with similar respect—a good sign.

Beside me, Evangeline breathed deep. Her brothers, Beth, Elise and Dallas all stood directly behind us, all with mixed emotions about her being front and center tonight. I admit, I might have been on the fence about it myself. However, the decision, just like *all* decisions concerning her life, was hers to choose.

"The sooner we get through this, the better," Declan said, leaning in so no one heard his thoughts but me.

I couldn't have agreed more, but did my best not to let it show.

With Nick's whereabouts still unknown, being out in the open like this wasn't ideal, but over the course of a few days, Evangeline had been different, less willing to let fear rule her. I'd witnessed her suddenly embracing her past—who she was in relation to who she still is—with open arms. The dreams were either the cause or a byproduct of this change, but I was certain the two were somehow related. It was almost as though, the old and new versions of her were beginning to collide.

She exhaled sharply again and glanced up toward me for reassurance. This one act required so much courage, causing pride to swell in my chest as she stepped forward to speak.

Each set of eyes focused intently on her. Some knew exactly who she was, others seemed bewildered. Still, they all likely *sensed* her authority because lycans were hardwired to instinctively feel the chain of command.

She stood in silence at first, but then opened her mouth and addressed the people.

Her people.

"Good evening," she began, her voice sounding small. "I know most of you don't really know who I am, but my name's Evie. My father's name was Noah and he was ruler of the original lycan clan that haled from Bahir Dar, Ethiopia. I haven't lived here long, but ... this place is home to me just as much as it is to the rest of you. For a long time, I wasn't sure what brought me to Seaton Falls, but I eventually came to realize that ... it was fate. Destiny." She paused and glanced around the crowd, meeting the gazes that stared back at her. "So many worked in secret to keep my identity hidden—even from me for a while," she joked, managing a smile despite her nerves.

"They worked to protect me and ensure the Sovereign didn't know I existed, because ... my family's a threat to him. I *am* a threat to him, to all he's built, to the fear he's trained us all to have toward him. Fear ... not respect."

She paused to gather herself, discreetly reaching for my hand.

"I'm sure that, like me, you're all tired of your lives being ruled by a tyrant. One who's all too willing to bring down his iron fist on anyone who dares to think for themselves, anyone who dares to say enough is enough, anyone who dares to put themselves and their families first. But ... isn't that what being a clan is about? Sensing the needs of the ones you love and pulling together as a community?"

The collective expressions of the people were beginning to shift. They were no longer confused as to why they'd been asked to come tonight. Before them, they witnessed a scared girl emerging as a queen.

And so did I.

"Once we defeat Sebastian—and we will defeat him—we'll step into a new day. Together," she declared. "From there forward, we will *all* be free."

A few cheers from the back spread forward until the entire crowd came alive.

"Yes, once we've dethroned the Sovereign and I've stepped into his place, there will still be order, but above all else there will be peace and fairness. I promise you that. Another vow I'm making to you here and now is that there will be no secrets wrapped in the guise of acting in your best interest. We will operate in the open with ample opportunity for each and every one of you to be heard."

There were more shouts and applause. This time, it went on for a bit and Evangeline had to wait for them to quiet down again. She'd hit a nerve. It became abundantly clear that this was one of their most prominent issues—being shuffled around like pawns, having no say when big decisions were made that affected them all.

"It's actually in the spirit of full disclosure that you were asked to come here today," Evangeline continued. "We've come into information that could have already affected us all, or will in the very near future. There's a chance the Sovereign has found a way to tap into the Elders' thoughts, a way to steal all our secrets, our defense strategy."

The sound of panicked whispers floated up from the crowd, but Evangeline didn't let it shake her.

"We only found out earlier this morning and wanted you all to know as soon as possible. And it is because of the Elders unknowingly being compromised that we must ask that you all no longer go to them with questions or to share personal information. Because, essentially, when you do this, you may as well be whispering those things right into the Sovereign's ear."

I watched her, noting how the timid voice she began this speech with was now gone. She spoke with confidence and they responded to that. Although the news she delivered was scary in too many ways to count, the people were not afraid because *she* was not afraid.

"We have to rely on each other more than we ever have. My family is here to help in any way we can, so please bring your concerns to us instead of the Elders and High Council. At least until we win this fight. As your future queen," she said with poise, "you have my word we'll do everything we can to ensure this clan arises victorious."

And just like that, by being exactly who she is, with no false airs or promises, she won the hearts of the people.

Declan, Ethan, and the others, moved into position, each stopping at one armory chest at a time. They opened them, inviting the clan to approach and take what they needed.

The sound of their applause and approval carried through the woods and there was no missing the look of pride on Elise's face. She was the only one, other than me, who'd had hundreds of years to think of Evangeline, to wonder what potential she could have reached had she not lost her life. For that reason, seeing her coming into her own present day was a miracle. It was as though nothing had been stolen, only delayed.

"Was that too presidential?" Evangeline whispered into my ear with a laugh.

I placed a kiss on the side of her face before answering. "It was perfect."

The hand she held was squeezed and I brought her close. It had been her call to go before the clan tonight and it was the *right* call.

Over the sound of ambient chatter, another sound caught my attention. It was the chirp of a walkie talkie. I turned, following the sound over my shoulder where Dallas had just lifted the device to listen.

"Dallas, got your ears on? Over," a voice called out.

"I'm here. Over."

"Yeah, uh ... a couple of the guys noticed something strange over near the main road. It's probably nothing, but they're going to check it out. Until we have clearance, it might be best for everyone to clear the area. Over," the guard suggested.

Right away, at the mention of there being a disturbance, my limbs and fists went rigid.

Dallas' gaze locked with mine and I knew we were of the same mind. We weren't willing to take any chances.

"Get Evie and Elise to the house safely," he instructed, "The boys and I will help get everyone else along as quickly as we can, and then join the team to see if they can use our help.

I nodded and turned to Evangeline. My entire life was, literally, all wrapped in the flesh of one woman. A woman who was standing here in the open, vulnerable.

"We've gotta move," I said, hearing the urgency in my own voice.

"Beth's coming with us. Her parents aren't here tonight," Evangeline said in a rush, her eyes widening as she reached for her friend's hand.

"Fine. We have to move quickly, though."

Elise nodded in agreement, keeping close as we moved toward the house.

Behind us, Dallas could be heard giving orders. He was doing his best to encourage those who remained to grab whatever weapons they needed, and then to head home. He then advised those still displaced by the flood and dwelling in the surrounding woods to seek refuge within the gates of our property. With the announcement, a mass of bodies formed behind us.

Most were doing well to conceal the fear that suddenly struck, but others weren't able to hide it. While, no, a threat hadn't been confirmed, this town had seen enough tragedy to know it was best to run at the first sign of smoke instead of waiting for a fire.

"I should go help them," Beth blurted, checking over her shoulder as chaos unfolded all around. "What if there really is something out there? The more manpower they have, the better, right?"

"The best thing any of us can do is follow the orders given by the guard," I explained.

I didn't want to feed the fight within her, but I could relate. It was unnatural for me to sit it out when comrades might need help, but it was even *more* unnatural to send Evangeline off alone. So, I forced myself to believe they had it under control, and kept walking.

But then we *all* stopped dead in our tracks, falling silent as we listened.

For a moment, I stood wondering if the sinister sound that emerged from the tree line was my imagination, but then a second unmistakable roar ripped through the air, confirming what I feared.

We weren't alone out here … and whatever had once been content to watch and wait, was now rushing right toward us.

I tightened my grip on Evangeline's hand as her other quickly latched on to Beth's arm. We ran—hard, fast, pressing harder as I think we all wished the house had been closer. While I had my doubts we'd be much safer inside the gate, I had to hope Hilda's sigils would hold. Had to hope they were strong enough to keep the unwanted, uninvited guests out.

Because this hope was all I had.

Within seconds, the scene surrounding us was utter chaos. I couldn't afford to look back.

"Elise, you'll have to sprint ahead," I called out. "Get the gate open. Otherwise, none of us will make it."

She nodded, agreeing before her body partially ignited and she took off. We were still a good enough distance from the house for it to be nerve wracking. Only more so when a cry from somewhere off to the right stole our attention. Someone who'd been running with us seconds before was taken out. Another scream to the left ended abruptly with a loud crunch and the sound of blood spurting from a fatal wound.

One by one, lycans were picked off and our group was shrinking.

"Mutt!" Beth called out, alerting me mere milliseconds before the thing was on me.

I managed to release Evangeline's hand just before being taken down to the ground. Deep gashes to my ribs from the thing's claws was the only damage I took before I ended the scuffle with a quick snap of its neck.

When I turned to search for Evangeline, I was grateful Beth had known to hold her back, only releasing her once I was on my feet and could take her hand.

We were on the move again. The encounter with the mutt had awakened the rage within me and both fists glowed red, heat spreading up my arms rapidly.

Arrows whizzed past our heads and the beat of heavy hooves came closer. Shadows weaved through the trees and my only thought was that I had to get her out of here, had to get her to safety if it was the last thing I did. The only plan I could come up with was to hide her.

All around us, the symphony of screams and death.

We were close, but they were closing in on us. A family of three had caught up and there was no missing the look of sheer terror on the father's face as he all but dragged his wife and daughter toward the same mark *we* aimed for.

With the wind whipping against her face and through her hair, Evangeline turned, noticing them mere seconds after I had. She didn't slow her pace, but she was clearly distracted. The dad's gaze locked on her, too, and his dark skin creased where tension spread across his forehead. His wife's pale cheeks were tinted red as she panted. Both clutched the hands of their little girl with tight, dark curls.

Looking at them, *really* looking at them, I understood why Evangeline had suddenly lost focus seeing this family.

They reminded her of her own.

She turned away, focusing straight ahead again, but I sensed that her energy had changed. Her thoughts were someplace else and I needed her to keep her head clear. We had to ...

"Mommy!"

The shrill cry that burst into the air sent a chill down my spine. Beside us, the family of three had just become two as a dark horse galloped away. On it's saddle, a lycan soldier with someone clutched beneath its arm.

And with the way the little girl screamed in horror, there was no guessing who that someone was.

"Mommy!" she cried out again.

Her father was clearly torn, his pace slowing as he struggled with two options—save my wife, or save my daughter.

My own heart ached with the difficult choice he faced.

"We have to do something," Evangeline muttered. The words left her mouth on autopilot. In her mind, that was simply a fact—*we had to do something.*

Beth passed me a concerned glance, but said nothing. She, too, may have recognized the resemblance of the trio that had been running beside us. It was also possible she worried that it might prompt Evangeline to act rashly.

"There's no time," I urged, keeping her at my side as our feet pounded the soil.

If it'd just been me, I would have gone after the woman without a second thought, even if it cost me my *own* life. But I wasn't as ready and willing to die for a stranger these days. Maybe because I finally had something to live for again.

"That little girl," Evangeline reasoned, "she just watched her mother get snatched away, Liam! We can't just let that happen."

There was so much conviction in her tone, it could be felt. Her heart was big, sometimes to a fault, but ... this felt like more than that. This felt personal. Like, seeing the girl's mother being taken away had hit a little too close to home.

Which was the only plausible reason I could conceive for what she did next.

The warmth of her hand in mine left so quickly I hardly had time to process it. However, my heart wasn't so slow to react. It raced as I held my breath and watched her take off in the wrong direction.

Toward danger.

CHAPTER 14

Liam

"Evangeline!"

She didn't respond and there was no time to think. Instead, my body simply reacted, going up in flames as I leapt into the air, bursting into flight. I thought I might stand a better chance of getting a visual on where she'd taken off to.

I couldn't lose her.

Not again.

Mutts were everywhere. Even more than I first realized. I called out to her again, but there was no diverting this mission of hers.

Not when I was certain she'd imposed her own experiences, her own emotions and loss on this little girl who was about to lose her mother.

An arrow whizzed past and I dodged it at the last moment, hearing another half a second later. Things were heating up and I tried not to think of what an ugly turn they'd taken. Tried not to think of how, in a matter of seconds, our night had gone from the extreme high of a successful rally, to ... this.

Just beneath me, Beth moved at top speed, hurdling obstacles in the underbrush, pushing as hard as she could to catch up to Evangeline. If I hadn't known the measure of her loyalty before, I would have now, seeing how she was nearly as desperate to end this chase as I was.

This had to end.

And fast.

I focused, keeping an eye on Evangeline through the trees, seeing only her silhouette as she gained on the intended target. A target I prayed she never reached. If she did, if the soldier wasn't willing to relinquish the woman ... it wouldn't end well.

Bright light to the east made my eyes dart that way, spotting the distinct outline of wings engulfed in flames. My guess was that Dallas had noticed me and came to see what sort of trouble I'd gotten myself into. Another set of eyes was a good thing, someone to help me take on whatever and *whoever* I had to.

She was so incredibly stubborn. I understood she had the best intentions, but sometimes I hated the depth of her nobility, the fact that she seemed to lose all sense of self-preservation when it came to someone else being in need.

I turned toward her again, noting that, now, mere feet separated her from the two on horseback. If I landed just right, I could come down on top of the soldier and wrangle him to the ground.

If ...

It felt like a missile torpedoed into me, blasting the broadside of my ribs, causing flames to explode outward from the blow. It only took a second to realize the dragon I'd seen barreling toward me wasn't one I knew, wasn't Dallas coming to help me stop Evangeline.

Hence this violent attempt to take me down.

Our bodies—mine and that of this traitorous dragon loyal to the Sovereign—rolled through the air, neither's mass unyielding to the other's as earth and sky tumbled around us. The moment I got my bearings, my fist connected with his face, and with the second it took him to recuperate, I was able to glance down, hoping I'd see Evangeline, but ... only darkness.

With my attention averted to search, the rogue dragon landed a hit of his own, connecting with the side of my face. However, the groan he let out right after was a clear sign he'd underestimated me. I'd always been resilient, maybe even more than the average shifter, but since being brought back, that strength had increased.

Without a second to spare, I gripped the fist he'd just broken against my jaw and crushed it in my palm. His voice rang out into the night, and with a swift headbutt between his eyes, I was able to knock him unconscious. His lifeless body plummeted, freefalling to the ground at high speed.

I scanned the underbrush in a panic, hoping to spot Evangeline or maybe Beth still chasing after her, but there was nothing. Only a feeling—our tether. It was still strong, so that brought me some sense of relief just knowing she was still alive, but I wasn't satisfied not having eyes on her.

'Evangeline, stop.'

I hoped to reason with her when I wandered inside her head, but she resisted.

'I can't just let them take her, turn her into a mutt, or ... worse,' she reasoned. 'Did you see the look on that little girl's face? She's just a kid. She needs her mom, Liam."

It became abundantly clear she wouldn't budge. My only choice was to find her and help her take down the soldier.

I dropped lower, just above the branches, weaving among them when I decided to land. The light of my flames illuminated the area and I had a glimpse of her now. Just barely.

Beth caught up, matching my speed.

"I tried, but she's too fast," she yelled.

It was true. Adrenaline and pure determination, had made Evangeline impossible to catch. Or it may have been something else. Descendants were among the most powerful shifters on Earth. Until now, she'd fallen short of her nature, the scope of her abilities. Whatever was awakening within her had seemingly triggered her inner strength to emerge as well.

Hence the reason she was gaining on her target while Beth and I were losing ground on ours.

A loud thud rang out, and then the distressed cry of a horse echoing off the trees. Up ahead, bodies tumbled on the ground and I knew she succeeded. The seconds it took me to reach the brawl were pure hell, wondering if she'd fair well against one of Sebastian's minions. We made it about halfway when I realized someone was missing—the woman. My fleeting guess was that she'd counted the distraction a blessing and sprinted toward her husband and child the moment the soldier was focused on someone other than herself.

Evangeline had done it. She'd created the diversion she intended to in order to free the woman. While I was certain there would be an ecstatic little girl leaping into her mother's arms in a moment, I wasn't sure any of us would be so pleased with this outcome.

"She's got him pinned down!" Beth announced.

I focused my eyes and finally made out the same scene. Evangeline had the soldier on his stomach, using her weight to hold him in the dirt. She yelled out in pure rage as she sank her fingers into his side, getting a grip on one of his thick ribs before snapping it free with ease.

The sound of his voice when he cried out into the night told of his agony.

She stayed on him, her hands locking beneath his head as she pulled. Pulled with everything in her as she grunted with the force she applied. It was enough to snap the soldier's neck, relieving us all when the apparent threat was no longer.

Beth panted beside me when we slowed to a stop. I, on the other hand, was not even winded. Evangeline slumped against a tree, fatigued from the fight.

"Are you hurt?" I asked in a rush, quickly kneeling when I was at her side.

"I'm fine," she nodded, catching her breath. "Did she ... did the woman get away?"

Her priorities hadn't shifted in the least. This question made that clear.

"I didn't see her, but I think so," I answered. "Hopefully, she makes it to the house, but there's no way to know."

And, I didn't say this part out loud, but even if she did make it, there was still no guarantee our home hadn't been compromised. The thought made me glance around, taking in our surroundings. We were alone for now, but that could change in an instant.

"We need to go," I asserted, gripping Evangeline beneath her arm.

Beth agreed with a nod. With Evangeline on her feet, we started back in our original intended direction, but what I feared came to pass within a few steps. The quiet stretch of woods we stood in a moment ago was now crawling with mutts, soldiers, more dragons ... and witches. With so many seeming to manifest out of thin air, I questioned whether we had been surrounded the entire time, their presence hidden by a charm.

Like ... a trap.

The pieces began to fit together—how the small family had so closely resembled Evangeline's, how the soldier chose to take the woman instead of the man to turn into a mutt, instead of taking the child to sire, how the woman had seemingly vanished into thin air the moment Evangeline reached them.

This ... it was the work of witches. I figured it out, but unfortunately, much, *much* too late.

My chest heaved with labored breath, taking in the breadth of the situation. We were grossly outnumbered—three of us to nearly thirty of them. The witches had already begun the work of suppressing my powers. It could be felt, the added weight on my limbs, weakening me as much as they could with my increased strength. Even my flames dimmed a bit, but there was still a hue of red engulfing my skin, my hair where it rested on my shoulders.

Other than distant screams and cries for help, this circle of the woods was eerily quiet. So quiet I heard the heavy footsteps trudging through the soil long before there was a face to go along with it. But then there was, and at the sight of Blaise, my flames glowed bright again, resisting the witches' magic.

Confused, they passed fleeting glances toward one another as their stench wafted in the breeze.

Blaise approached, first settling his attention on me, the red of my flames that stood out in comparison to the dragons that had aligned with them in this fight. His gaze did a quick sweep, scanning me from head to toe, taking in my size as I towered over the others in my shifted form. There was a brief moment of confusion, but that look was replaced by another as his gaze passed over to Evangeline. Now, all that remained was a dark smile.

My fists clenched and my thoughts turned morbid, focused on this war ending once and for all with Blaise and Sebastian both meeting a gruesome, untimely end.

Blaise closed the distance between him and Evangeline. My mind signaled my limbs to move, to step in between them, but the magic made this impossible. Instead, I was forced to be a spectator.

"Don't take another step," I warned, the words leaving my mouth as more of a growl as they hissed from between my teeth.

"Or what?" Blaise mocked, that grin of his widening as he eyed me again. When I began to struggle against his witches' spell, he released a bored sigh. "Relax. I won't be hurting your beloved today. It's recently come to our attention that she's far more valuable to us alive than dead," he explained, adding, "for now."

He was nearly face-to-face with her now and I noted how she tensed. When she passed a quick glance my way, I was certain she had attempted to communicate via our thoughts, but the spell had likely jammed up our frequency on my end, seeing as how it couldn't affect *her*.

Blaise's sights were set on me again after walking a slow circle around Evangeline, staring with that dead look that always dwelled behind his eyes.

"Looks like we win again, dragon," he laughed, signaling over his shoulder for a handful of his soldiers to step forward. "Tie her up and head east. The others are waiting for us. Bring the blonde, too," he added. "I'm sure I'll find some use for her."

With that command issued, the soldiers began the ascent on Evangeline and Beth, both beginning to shift, thinking their best bet was to fight in their true form.

"Don't ... even think about it," Blaise called out, leveling a glare on them both. "Shift and I'll finish what we started with your dragon."

His gaze came back to me and so did that smile I wanted to rip from his face. "This is a good look for you," he commented, adding, "The new wings and all."

His smirk fueled my rage and I felt the magic beginning to slip. It wasn't strong enough to hold me forever. Not like before. Not as bits of the memories from the time I spent with Sebastian and Blaise splintered into my thoughts.

Blaise turned to Evangeline and Beth one last time. "Are we clear on the rules, ladies?" he asked.

I locked gazes with Evangeline and could pinpoint the moment she saw the situation for exactly what it was. Hopeless. At the sight of it, that look, my heart broke in a million pieces. She eventually nodded, agreeing to this bastard's terms because her back was against a wall.

"Glad to hear it," he crooned, tipping his chin to signal his men to carry on.

"Are we taking the dragon, too?" one soldier asked.

Blaise, without hesitation, gave his next order. "As amused as Father would be to see the upgrades he's acquired since his brief stint as a human, I'm going to do us all a favor. This one is quite vicious when left to his own devices. Let's just put an end to this once and for all."

Sweat poured down my face and neck as I fought the spell, as hard as I could, feeling the strain of tendons and veins as I pushed my dragon to it's limits. This ... what they were trying to do ... it couldn't happen. They couldn't take her from me.

Couldn't take *them* from me—my love, my ... child.

"You should know something before you die, Reaper," Blaise said, casting one final look my way as his men closed in on me. "We've got the Liberator with us, too."

When I managed to press forward a few feet, fighting the spell, Blaise's brow twitched.

"Settle down. We're working on a way to keep both alive. And, if our sovereign king succeeds, rest assured the child won't be fatherless," he grinned sinisterly. "We'll raise the little brat up like one of our own. And with a bit of our influence, he or she will one day be the greatest weapon this world has ever known. You can count on that."

With so few words, Blaise had just made my worst fear a reality.

CHAPTER 15

Evie

They knew exactly how to separate me from the herd, knew my weakness was family. Or more specifically, knew my weakness was having my family ripped from me.

But it was easy because they knew me, knew *all* of us. I suppose spying through the Elders' and Hilda's thoughts provided the Sovereign quite the advantage.

I originally thought the soldier had come out of nowhere, snatching this woman from her daughter's grasp. Seeing it, my heart was nearly torn from my chest. I'd seen the look that little girl wore before—in the mirror on my own face. It was still fresh in my memory what it was like for a parent to suddenly be gone, how helpless that felt. I couldn't, in good conscience, standby and let a child feel that.

Only ... there wasn't really a child, wasn't really a woman.

Only the work of witches and their clever illusions. Apparently, their magic didn't work on me, but I was susceptible to their manifestations just like everyone else.

Blaise had two soldiers inject Beth and I with something the moment we were shoved inside a dark van waiting on the outskirts of the woods. Once the injection took effect, our wrists and ankles were bound with heavy chains. Whatever the syringe contained made it hard to focus on any one thought, any particular face or conversation. It all ran together in a blur. Still, my thoughts managed to settle on Liam.

I tried desperately to communicate with him before being taken away, but the witches must have blocked him. This, too, had been a disadvantage of being watched, of them knowing each of our abilities like the back of their hands.

With the scene that unfolded as we were taken away, I would have thought they killed him, but ... I still felt him. So strong. It was my hope that, once whatever spell the witches had cast to separate our mental connection had faded, I'd be able to speak to him again.

I was worried—about him, the family, the clan. I hadn't even had time to process how bad things had gotten in just a matter of minutes.

There was a sound just outside the van, and then a flash of light that filtered in beneath the door.

"Evie, we can't let them separate us," Beth grumbled, clearly feeling just as groggy as I did. "We have to stay together. It's the only way I can protect you and the baby."

I reached for her hand beside me and held on, the closeness to my best friend being my only comfort. She'd taken off running right behind me as I chased after the woman. In this instance, Beth's loyalty had come back to bite her. Although, I was almost certain she wouldn't see it that way. Like she said, she was determined to protect us.

The back doors of the van unlatched, and then flung open. Behind two massive silhouettes were the headlights of a second vehicle.

"Out," came a hard voice.

They didn't wait for Beth and I to get to our feet before grabbing us each by our arms and snatching us toward the back bumper, and then to the dirt.

"Careful."

I glanced left to spot Blaise's boots, realizing he'd been the one to bark the command at the rough soldier.

"This one's carrying precious cargo," he added as he approached, pointing a finger toward me. His feet stopped and the headlights illuminated the dust he kicked up on his walk closer.

He stopped where I rested on all fours on the ground, and when he extended a hand, I flinched, remembering our last encounter. I'd been jabbed with that awful cattle prod of his, sending electricity all through my body, causing pain I didn't even know was possible. In fact, had it not been for Liam's dragon suddenly awakening, I would have died beneath Blaise's boot that day.

My gaze lifted to meet his. Without accepting his help, I stood to my feet, hearing the thick chains I'd been placed in rattle with each movement.

Blaise smiled and stood upright again. "Very well then."

He didn't bother offering the same to Beth as she, too, stood to her feet, knowing it would only earn him another rejection.

"We've just got a short walk ahead of us," he said jovially.

At his command, the soldiers moved swiftly—most escorting us up the side of a steep, rugged hill, the others hopping back inside the two vans before continuing on down the road.

I had no idea where we were, how long we'd driven. I suppose that had been the point of dosing us. Well, that and the fact that we would have given the guards hell the entire way here. Even if it proved to be our last fight.

Beth passed a look my way and I noticed she didn't seem as incoherent as before. I, too, felt clearer in thought and used that to my advantage, searching for any landmarks or details that might tell me where we were. When my eyes found hers again, she did a quick glance toward one of the soldiers and mine did the same, settling on something visible in his back pocket.

A knife.

The chains on my wrist were heavy, but getting lighter by the second, as the substance we'd been given wore off.

I swallowed hard, knowing that once we reached our destination, the odds of escaping were slim to none.

It had to be now.

Right now.

My thoughts aligned and I saw each action I took half a second before moving. Energy pulsed through my fingers as I prepared to lunge forward.

"I'd think twice about that if I were you," Blaise growled, his voice breaking my concentration *and* foiling my plan to stab one of his men.

It might have been the last chance of escape Beth and I had.

"My *father* may think you're more valuable alive than dead, but make no mistake," he warned, "I am not my father."

Heat blazed in my neck and face. I hated him. For too many reasons to name. He seemed to sense this and smirked before barking a command at the soldiers leading Beth and I by our chains.

"Keep moving."

We walked for miles, leaving the road quite some time ago. When we neared our destination, blindfolds were placed over our eyes and we stumbled our way onto pavement again. My only visual reference was my shoes through the sliver of open space beneath the material. The uncertainty was enough to raise my heartrate a little.

"Inside," Blaise ordered.

A second later, a heavy, metal door screeched open and we crossed a threshold. Our footsteps echoed throughout, bouncing off unseen surfaces as Beth and I were led in. I could hear her breaths coming as quickly as my own. We were completely at the mercy of these men, and I couldn't think of a worse scenario.

"Get them to the cell," Blaise ordered.

The soldiers leading us didn't ask questions, just followed directions. My wrists were tugged, pinching in the links of the chains that bound us. The pain was only a slight distraction from everything else—fear, regret, defeat.

A hard shove to my back and I tripped into the small space they brought us to. The blindfolds we wore were snatched from our eyes and I stood face to face with one of the guards as he retrieved a key from his pocket, unlocking my ankles, and then my wrists.

He backed away, waiting for his comrade to free Beth, and then both turned to leave the cell of what I could only guess to be an abandoned prison. And judging by the specs of the room—size, extensive security measures, single barred window—we were in solitary confinement.

The sound of the door being slammed shut was jarring, because of the startling noise, yes, but mostly because we had no clue what Sebastian had planned for us.

Outside the door, footsteps shuffled, some going quieter, others growing louder. I turned toward Beth and there were no words, there was no plan. All we could do was cleave to each other, so that's what we did. My hand went into hers and we moved toward the back wall.

I could feel her shaking beside me and I was certain she could feel the same. While I wished she'd been able to get away, I was eternally grateful I wasn't alone here.

The sound of a voice startled a gasp from my throat.

"What a lovely surprise," the visitor crooned.

With the structure of the door, there was only a small peep-hole up top meant for someone to see in, not for us to see out. Our only visual of the person who spoke was a small, waist-high slit where I guessed meals were meant to be exchanged. Through it, a black jacket could be seen, hands folded in front, a gaudy ring on one hand as the head of a cane pressed into his palm.

Still, even with so little to go on, I'd know that voice anywhere ... *Sebastian*.

"I do hope my men weren't too rough. They're used to dealing with the more rugged variety of shifter, not the likes of a queen," he expressed. There was an air of mockery in his tone. "And I see you've brought a friend with you this time."

At his words, Beth inched closer to my side.

"No need to be afraid, little wolf," he laughed. "My son seems to be intrigued by you, so I can almost guarantee your safety as much as Evangeline's. Assuming you're ... accommodating."

I felt my stomach turn, but held my composure because I was certain he watched us through that peephole, waiting to see us squirm.

My lips parted, and I'd just gotten my thoughts together to try reasoning with this man—a tyrant—but then there was a sound. A sound that silenced me after uttering only one syllable.

It was a roar, one that echoed from ... *everywhere*.

Beth spoke up before I had the chance. "What was that?" As soon as the words left her mouth, she was on guard.

"Oh, what a pity he spoiled it. I was so looking forward to you *seeing* my surprise as opposed to just hearing it, but I suppose the cat is out of the bag now," he teased, the sound of amusement marking his tone. "We have another interesting guest and I believe the two of you are actually very well acquainted. And, judging by how excited he is all of a sudden, I'm guessing he knows you're here."

From the other side of the door, Sebastian bellowed a dark laugh. It was the laugh of a man who got off on toying with the lives of others, a man who enjoyed playing the role of puppeteer. It was the laugh of a man who thought nothing of bringing me here, under the same roof as the one who wanted nothing as much as he wanted me dead.

"She can't be here with him," Beth forced out, putting her own fears aside to speak up for me. "Your son mentioned that you want her kid, right? You have some sort of ... plans for it, I'm guessing? Well, I can guarantee that if you don't move him or move *us* ... she'll never make it."

Sebastian was still as a statue where we saw him through the slit in the door. "It's being taken care of," was his only response, so casual as our lives hung in the balance.

"I'll return to check in later," he promised.

One I hoped to God he didn't keep.

"Oh ... and I took the liberty of making certain those handy little flames of yours couldn't do a number on *these* doors like they did on the last. You taught me quite the lesson after your nifty little parlor trick up north. Thanks to you, we were able to better prepare this time around," he added, leaving us the next second.

Dim light filtered in through the slot his body once blocked. His footsteps, and those of a few soldiers, could be heard growing faint as the distance between them and us lengthened.

Beth slowly slid down the wall, sitting beside me again as we both soaked in the breadth of our circumstances.

In short, they were dire.

There was a fading hope in the back of my mind that someone would find us in time. With me only being able to *feel* Liam—but not being able to communicate with him, or sense his location—I couldn't say for certain he could get to us. Now we'd just discovered that Nick was here, too, and Sebastian was grossly underestimating what he was capable of.

"There has to be a way out," Beth sighed. "I'm gonna shift and see if I can ... I don't know ... tunnel through the walls. I'm guessing the witches put some kind of spell on this place if they're smart, but ... it's worth a try, right? Not to mention, it's the only shot we have."

After the statement, she braced her hands against the walls as if to gage their strength. I watched, not wanting to tell her how pointless this would be. I mean, it wasn't like *my* abilities would work to free us either. Thanks to Sebastian taking special precautions this time around.

Beth removed her shoes, reaching for the button of her jeans next as she prepared to shift, but a sound outside the cell door froze us both in place.

"You hear that?" she whispered, creeping toward the back wall again, maybe hoping to put as much space between us and whoever might have been coming to enter. Considering Sebastian and his brood, we could be certain the visitor had ill intentions.

The steps that approached were quiet, as if this person hoped to catch us off guard. Or maybe they'd been sent to eavesdrop. Either way, Beth and I were silent.

Even when a small piece of paper was dropped in through the slot and those same footsteps made quick work of darting away.

Beth and I exchanged a glance, both confused by what had just taken place, but I was too curious to just sit there. She was on my heels, watching over my shoulder as I grabbed the paper and unfolded it, reading the words in a whisper.

'I CAN HELP YOU.'

Neither of us had any idea who our wanna-be-savior was, or even if they were legit, but ... for now, they were the only hope we had.

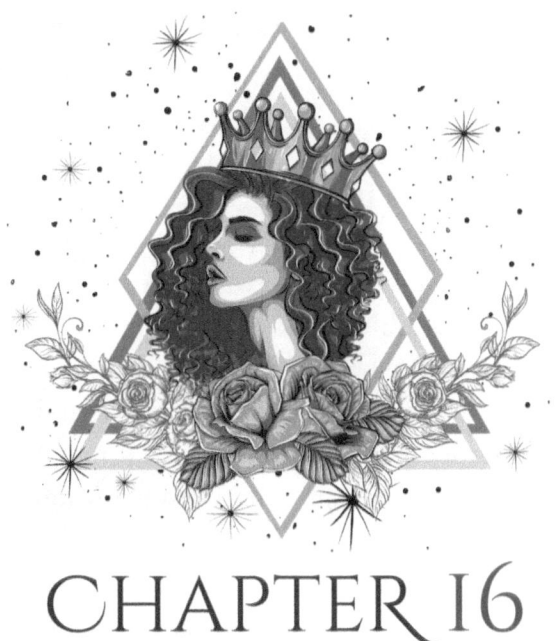

CHAPTER 16

Nick

There was rock bottom ... and then there was this.

The tendons beneath my arms stretched to capacity as the very tips of my toes swept across the concrete. Sweat poured from my face and neck, merging with *more* sweat as I hung from thick chains. The steal beams they attached to creaked and moaned with every move I made, feeling the burn from within as my body rejected this process.

This ... process.

Blood poured from my mouth as I vomited more of it up. It had been the only thing I was allowed to consume for days—all part of Sebastian's plan to sire me, to control me like some exotic pet. I overheard guards talking a few nights ago when I drifted into consciousness. Apparently, this is the Sovereign's hobby, collecting oddities within the supernatural world. It just so happened I was one such oddity.

Another?

A royal descendent—Evie.

I felt her the moment they brought her here, placing my weakness in a cell not nearly far enough away to keep her safe. That was nearly a week ago now, and every second of every day, all I could think about was killing her.

Sebastian came in to observe every so often, seemingly disappointed when he laid eyes on me, the darkness that flowed through my veins as murderous thoughts ravished me. I believed he thought I ought to have been past this craving by now, but if he felt what I felt on the inside, he would have known that was impossible. Despite the sire bond he hoped to establish beginning to take effect, I knew there would never be anything to override this feeling.

Nothing.

Ever.

A guard paced past the door where I was held, in what I imagined to have once been the cafeteria of a long-abandoned prison. The broken, overturned tables and steel-topped serving counter were a dead giveaway. Behind it, a dark kitchen that now lie dormant. I focused on the doorway again, watching as he passed for a second time.

Every second was grueling, wanting to break free from these chains and just ... find her. As ashamed as I was for feeling so weak by such a dark need, I was a slave to it.

"Hey!" I called out.

He ignored me, so I called out again.

"Come here a sec," I panted. Every breath was labored and painful as I struggled against the chains.

Heavy boots crushed small pieces of debris beneath them as he approached. Finally. He gazed up at me with a bored stare, making sure to keep his hand on his knife just in case I tried something.

"What?" he sighed.

I blinked through droplets of sweat that sat on the tips of my lashes. "I need to speak with Sebastian. Heck, I'll even settle for Blaise, but I need someone."

The guard looked me over quickly and scoffed before walking away. "Yeah, and I need a million bucks. Guess we'll both die disappointed," he grumbled.

"It's an emergency," I shouted back. "He brought a girl here, didn't he?"

My question made the guard's steps halt, but he didn't turn.

"A hybrid," I added. "He made a mistake, though. She can't be here with me. It's just a matter of time until I can't control this and I lose it. If that happens, these chains may as well be made of straw," I warned.

He seemed to get a kick out of that—me thinking I could break free.

"Oh, yeah? And who exactly is gonna help you?" he taunted. "Cause last I checked, you were locked down pretty good."

I didn't have time for this. "Get Sebastian," I demanded. "When he hears what I have to say, you might even get a gold star for being a good little pup." When I finished, I laughed, seeing that the comment had gotten under his skin.

He came close again, but this time it wasn't to talk. Instead, he pounded his fist into my gut and air rushed from my lungs, forcing more blood up from my stomach with it. As I writhed and coughed, he retreated again, keeping his gaze trained on me.

"Keep your mouth shut and this'll go a whole heck of a lot smoother for all of us," he warned, sending the rage within me through the roof.

Letting them keep me in these chains was getting harder by

the second and, soon, I wouldn't be able to keep the beast on its leash.

He'd be here soon, and when that happened, there wouldn't be a lycan or dragon alive who could stop him.

Not even me.

Liam

She was nowhere. Like she'd been wiped clean off the face of the Earth.

Only ... I knew that wasn't so because the tug at the center of my chest said otherwise. It'd been the only thing that kept me from losing myself completely after a full week since she'd been taken. It'd been the only way I knew for sure Nick hadn't gotten to her. However, we were on borrowed time in that respect, with Sebastian thinking it was a bright idea to hold Evangeline anywhere near the Liberator.

"We'll find her."

I paused, glancing up from the bag I packed to find Elise watching. Her eyes were rimmed red and there were dark circles underneath them. A week not knowing where her daughter was had been almost as heart-wrenching as it had been for me.

Almost.

I didn't respond because I was honestly out of things to say. Sebastian's witches had done a great deal to keep Evangeline hidden from me, to keep our connection severed. I hadn't slept in so long I was delirious, unable to form a coherent thought as I went over the night again and again, wondering how I let this happen.

Wondering how I failed.

Elise stepped closer and took a seat as I shoved a flashlight into the side pocket. She was quiet at first, and then decided to say more.

"It's not your fault," she insisted, speaking kindly as if wanting to avoid offsetting a trigger. "I've listened to you explain it to my boys, to Dallas, and there was nothing else you could have done. Evangeline took off because she thought she could help, thought it was the right thing to do, and the Sovereign exploited her heart's weakness," she explained. "If we're to be angry with anyone, it's Sebastian. Not ourselves."

I heard her, loud and clear, but there wasn't much she could say to convince me this wasn't on me. Therefore, I didn't deserve to be made to feel better. I needed to carry this pain and frustration at full force and use it to push me to find her.

I scoured the area all day and all night, every day and every night. We'd even been back to Ridge Borough several times, to the warehouse, hoping we'd find her, or at least someone we could torture an answer out of, but ... no one.

Every time, we came up empty.

I'd opted to spend nights out in the woods. Not only was there no time for sleep, I also couldn't imagine lying in my bed without her, knowing she was out there somewhere. I patrolled mostly, keeping an eye out for some of Sebastian's rogue soldiers or witches who might wander into the area looking for trouble. If they crossed paths with me, they were sure to find it. There wasn't much I wasn't willing to do to bring her back.

Hiking the bag onto my shoulder, I moved toward the stairs, taking them by two as I headed toward the front door. I had every intention to leave without responding to Elise's statement, but when I reached the foyer and her fingers linked around my wrist, my respect for her forced me to stop and listen.

"I only want to know that you have a plan," she sighed.

I didn't look her in her eyes because that deep stare reminded me too much of Evangeline's.

"My only plan is the same as it's always been—I'll find the bastards who took her, and then ... I'll kill them. End of story," I seethed. "But I don't have time to talk. The guys are still out there searching and the Stokes's are on their way. I only came in to re-up on supplies before the sun sets, so ..."

"I understand that, but ... what happens next, after you've found her? What of the soldiers? The witches? More specifically, the one who cast the spell on the weapon that injured Ivan?"

She threw all these questions at me and I knew she was right to worry about the execution of our plan. However, I wasn't exactly in the right frame of mind to answer. I was unhinged to say the least. Every thought in my head was dark, every feeling was of causing someone pain, so, no, I didn't have the details worked out.

"Liam," she pressed, "I'm asking for your word that you aren't just roaming around out there from sunup to sundown like some madman with nothing to lose."

"There *is* nothing left to lose!" I shouted. "Not anymore. The one thing I did have to live for has been taken from me ... *again, Elise.* So, no, having some mapped out script to follow isn't exactly top priority at the moment, because all I can think about is her. All I *want* is her," I breathed, feeling like I'd reached my breaking point.

When I slumped and took a seat on the bottom step, Elise didn't let my outburst push her away. She knew me like she knew *all* her children and, instead, sat right beside me. She knew the one thing that could make me come undone at the seams was her daughter, and that was the exact effect this week apart had on me.

Her hand was warm against my back and it was only some-what comforting. It was nice to have her sympathy, but changed nothing.

"I'm sorry," she said softly. "Dallas mentioned you all had done some strategizing during your search last night. I just thought that ... maybe you'd come up with a way to settle things once and for all."

She was tired—tired of worrying about her family, tired of

having to question who could be trusted. I understood that because we shared the same sentiment.

"I might have a solution, but I can almost guarantee you won't like it," Dallas cut in, surprising Elise and I both when he stepped into the foyer.

"What do you mean?" Elise piped up, turning to face him now.

"It would put us on a very strict timeline, adding pressure to an already tense situation, but ... I think we would all be willing to take a risk or two if it means putting this war behind us," he shared.

"Absolutely, but what sort of risk are we talking here?"

He sighed before answering Elise's question. "Well, to start, we need Hilda and the Elders, which will mean Sebastian can easily spy our plan if we don't move quickly, before he does that little ... head-hopping thing Hilda explained to us. If we move too fast, we can get ourselves in a heap of hot water. Move too slowly and Sebastian will see it coming and use our plan against us," Dallas explained. "So, we've got to do this just right. Timing is everything."

Elise was on her feet the next instant. "I'll get Hilda back here right away and I'm certain the Elders will cooperate as long as what we propose is in the best interest of the clan."

She left us the next second to make arrangements.

With Elise out of the room Dallas and I were left on our own. And it was then I realized there was more, something else he maybe hadn't wanted to mention in front of her.

"What is it?" I asked.

He peered up and, being a soldier at heart, he made quick work of concealing his emotions again.

"I didn't want to get Elise's hopes up, but there's been new info," he started. "The kid I told you about, the one we snuck into Sebastian's camp—he's been busy."

My brow tensed. I recalled him mentioning something like

that during our first mission to Ridge Borough, but honestly hadn't given it much thought since then. A Damascus Facility student had been recruited to act as our eyes and ears among Sebastian's men. Until now, that was *all* we knew, but apparently Dallas was about to change that.

"He saw them," Dallas whispered. "Evie, Beth. They've been in Ridge Borough since the night Blaise and the gang passed through."

But ... that didn't make sense. We'd checked there several times, combing every inch of woods, every street and alley. Was it possible that we missed them?

Seeing my mind reel, Dallas interjected to say more.

"Before you ask, it's a spell. The kid says Sebastian's got a whole *army* of witches and they live for the sadistic tasks he gives them. So, we could have gone there a million and nine times and *still* would have come up empty."

"I need the exact location," I said in a rush, feeling like this sudden sense of urgency would eat me alive if I didn't move.

"Easy now," Dallas piped. "Since we've got ourselves a bonafied plan for once, we have to be careful. We stand to make a real mess of things if we aren't smart. One stupid move and the whole plan's shot to hell."

I heard him and understood the stakes, but couldn't accept what he proposed, that we just ... wait. When I took a step toward the door, his hand planted firm in the center of my chest.

"Whoa, whoa ... did you hear what I said?" he asked, his expression turning sympathetic when his gaze landed on me.

I was desperate and beyond having enough pride to hide it. I was a broken man, one on the verge of self-destruction.

His hand fell away, but he held my gaze.

"We have to give ourselves the best possible chance of succeeding, Liam. And as hard a pill as this is for you to swallow ... the way to save Evangeline is not to storm into Sebastian's town like a runaway train," he reasoned. "Getting her out unharmed is gonna take stealth, precision, and wisdom. Any of those elements goes lacking and the whole thing blows up in our faces."

I couldn't fathom his request. It *sounded* like he expected me to wait, wanted me to leave Evangeline out there while we waited for all the pieces to fit together.

I shook my head as words tumbled from my mouth. "I can't … just … stop looking for her," I breathed.

It didn't matter that I knew magic hid her and going in alone would be an impossible task. The only thing that registered was that I now had confirmation of the general area where she'd been taken. At the moment, that sounded like more than enough.

Dallas didn't budge. "Under normal circumstances, I'd never expect you to wait," he sympathized, "but you know what we're up against. We need every ace we've got if we stand a chance at pulling this off. So, if you rush in, guns blazing and blow the roof off the entire operation … there's no guarantee you'll be able to get her out of this, no guarantee we'll take down his entire army, no guarantee we'll get what we need to help Ivan."

His reasoning would have made perfect sense to a sane man. Only, I didn't exactly meet those specifications at the moment.

My fists were clenched tight. For the most part, I didn't disagree with his logic, but my heart wasn't giving in as easily. It couldn't seem to settle on the idea of more time passing, more time away from her.

Dallas and I stood facing one another in the foyer at a stalemate when Elise returned. The look of accomplishment she wore made it clear things on her end had gone according to plan.

"Well, I managed to get a call in to Hilda and she'll be here by midnight."

"And the Elders?" Dallas asked, finally pealing his eyes away from me.

"I radioed one of the guards with a message and he says Baz

and the Chancellor will see us. We'll head over as soon as Hilda gets in," she answered.

"Good," he sighed. "This is exactly what we need." He glanced at me again and I knew what he was thinking—that if I would just settle down, would just let him work out whatever plan he devised, this would all go more smoothly.

My heart beat wildly in my chest, knowing there were mere miles between Evangeline and I.

Elise gaged the tension that volleyed between Dallas and I before asking a question. "Did I miss something?"

I stood like a statue, saying nothing, but Dallas' rationale had gotten to me. If there was a way to increase our odds of getting Evangeline out safely ... I'd be crazy not to try.

The instant he saw my shoulders lose tension, the moment he saw my brow relax, he breathed a sigh of relief knowing I'd comply.

"Nope, everything's all good," he finally said, answering Elise's question. "I'm gonna radio the boys and tell them to come in so we can brief them."

Elise seemed content with that as she turned to leave us again.

"One day," Dallas said quietly. "Give it one day to make sure things are done the right way, to make sure we kill this problem at the root."

My heart ached in a way it never had before, knowing the sun would set again before I could go after her, but ... there was no other option. As much as I hated to admit it, this problem was bigger than me and I'd need those around me to help fix it.

So, feeling completely defeated, I agreed to his terms.

"One day."

CHAPTER 17

Evie

They were all here—Liam, my brothers.

I wasn't sure if this dream of them was just because my heart, literally, ached for them, or maybe it was another of the vivid memories breaking through. Either way, after a week away from home, I welcomed it, welcomed the feeling of being surrounded by love and family again.

I glanced around a large table, staring at each of their faces, feeling the closeness. Beside me, Ivan could barely get a statement out, laughing hard with a mouth full of food. I smiled, half-listening as I discreetly stared across the table at the new object of my obsession.

Liam.

Our love felt new and old at the same time.

New, because I was certain this memory was from shortly after he'd come to my room and we succumbed to our desires.

Old, because I was certain I'd always loved him.

Maybe even before our souls were contained in physical bodies —like Hilda suggested.

I popped a grape into my mouth and tried to focus on only Ivan when he asked why I'd suddenly gotten quiet.

"I um ... my apologies. I'm a bit tired," I explained. "I didn't get much sleep last night."

There was a fleeting image that flashed in my thoughts—one of a silhouette being cast by candlelight onto the stone wall of my bedroom. It only took a moment to realize that silhouetted figure was Liam's. A glimpse from yet another passionate night we'd had in secret.

At the memory, I swallowed hard, extending my hand toward a metal chalice filled with wine.

The table was silent and I glanced around to see why my brothers had suddenly run out of things to say. Their gazes were shifted from me to Liam and back again. There were smirks, too, an at the sight of them, my stomach sank.

"Didn't get much sleep ... " Josiah said thoughtfully, bearing his teeth when he smiled.

My throat felt tight and a trickle of sweat raced down the center of my back.

He turned to Liam and asked a follow-up question. "Did you get a good night's rest, brother?"

I pushed my chair away from the table and dropped the napkin I held beside my fork. "If you don't mind, I think I'll finish my meal in my bedroom," I announced, doing little to hide that this was an exit strategy, doing my best to get away before the accusations began to fly. I was certain my brothers knew exactly what Liam and I had been up to, but weren't gracious enough to pretend they didn't.

"And uh ... will Liam be joining you up there? Perhaps for

dessert?" Tobias asked next—this question being the straw that broke the camel's back. They exploded with laughter and I could feel my face warming.

"You're disgusting," I accused, doing all I could to deflect. "All of you."

I cast a look toward Liam who, smiling, took another healthy bite from the leg of lamb he held in his fist. He wasn't bothered or embarrassed in the least, but hadn't confirmed any of my brothers' charges.

I took a step, but Declan had my wrist. "Don't run off, Evangeline. We didn't mean to embarrass you," he said sweetly. "It wouldn't be right if we didn't give you two a hard time about this."

I stood there a moment, my chest and shoulders heaving after having been humiliated, but then I settled into my seat again. Ivan grabbed my hand and squeezed it when he smiled.

I was quiet, moving food around my plate, but not bothering to eat. My stomach was too topsy-turvy to even try.

My brothers had gone silent, too. And that was, perhaps, the most unnerving part. I was used to them being a boisterous bunch, so this strange behavior had set my nerves on edge.

Frustrated, I let out a sigh and dropped my fork to the plate, eyeing each of them.

"Just ... say whatever it is you have to say," I urged. "The quicker we get this over with, the quicker we can move on."

I sat, waiting, but none of them spoke.

"Seriously? First, you couldn't seem to keep your snide remarks to yourself. Now, you're suddenly all out of things to say? Unbelievable ..." I scoffed.

"Calm down," Ethan chuckled. "You know how we feel about Liam. He's as much a part of our family as anyone else sitting at this table. None of us could think of a better man to love and care for you, our one and only sister."

A smile followed the statement and some of the hostility I built up toward them faded.

A little, anyway.

"Have either of you thought of how you'll break the news to Father?"

It was Caleb who asked, and all eyes darted toward him. While the current me had no recollection of what Noah was like as a father, the version of myself in this memory felt a spike in her heartrate. I guessed that meant she was at least mildly concerned how he'd react.

"There's no reason to tell him," I blurted.

Caleb erupted with laughter and I stared at him. "Are you insane? Noah believes it is his God-given right and his duty to know everything that goes on in his kingdom. So what makes you think he won't be angry if something beneath this very roof goes on without his knowing?"

"And what's so difficult about it?" Ivan jumped in again. "You'll only be telling him one of his sons has been ... intimate ... with his beloved daughter, the jewel in his crown. Nothing odd about that, right?"

The crass phrasing made me uncomfortable, my expression shifted to match.

"Yes, Liam is family, and like a son to him, a brother to you six, but ... I've never looked at him that way," I shared. The part of that I didn't admit out loud was that I never looked at him in that light because, even as a little girl, I felt something for him.

Love that was not familial in nature.

I cleared my throat after pondering that for a moment, deciding it was too personal to share.

"Oh, I can hear the rumors now," Ethan laughed. "Scandal in the palace," he added, stating the words as though they would be the headline of some newspaper.

Or ... whatever people relied on for news updates back then.

"How did you all know anyway?" I asked, finally feeling settled enough to give eating another try. I'd just bitten into an apple when Tobias answered.

"The same way Mother and Father would have known if they had the misfortune of their bedroom being in the same wing as yours."

His response made me swallow before I meant to, and the chunk of fruit in my mouth went down the wrong way. I reached for my wine again as they all shared a laugh at my expense.

Brothers ...

"At first, I thought you'd snuck an outsider in. Naturally, I woke the others to storm into your bedroom and toss the bastard over the balcony, but ... then we went to get Liam. Finding his bed empty was somewhat of a clue," Ethan smiled suggestively, bouncing his brow with the gesture. "It didn't take us long to figure it out."

The embarrassment quickly returned as I imagined what they'd done after realizing what had gone on in my room ... and with whom. They had probably gathered outside my door, listening, getting the laugh of a lifetime at my expense.

"Usually, we only ever hear racket like that coming from Declan's room," Ethan chuckled, nudging Caleb in the arm.

"Then perhaps you ought to spend less time eavesdropping and more time taking notes," Declan replied, causing the others to laugh. And even I cracked a smile.

The conversation took a turn then, transitioning to my six brothers comparing stats of their own love lives, and I didn't feel so strange having this conversation anymore. Above the chatter, the laughter, I caught Liam's stare. Another smile broke free and there was no containing it. He just brought out this softer side of me and ... so help me God ... I loved it.

Loved him.

I reveled in this feeling, wishing it would never end, but it was inevitable that I'd be thrust back into reality, back into the cell *where I'd spent so many terrifying days. The fabric of the vision broke apart and I felt the loss immediately, realizing right away that my surroundings hadn't changed. Much to my dismay, I was still trapped in Sebastian's hell.*

As I blinked, the four walls confining Beth and I to this small space seemed so much closer, as if they were shrinking around us. She was asleep beside me on the lone mattress that had been shoved in here on our third day, saving us from spending another night on the cold, hard, cement floor. We couldn't say for sure, but we both wondered if this was a gift that had been arranged by our anonymous angel. Whoever he or she might have been.

I closed my eyes and tried to hold onto the dream that had just teased me with a hint of freedom, hoping for sleep, but ... there was a pain. One so swift and so sharp I cried out into the night.

It was blinding, making me forget where I was in that moment.

Beth sat straight up, turning toward me as I continued to cry out in pain.

"What is it? What happened?" she asked in a panic, placing a hand on my back as I doubled over.

The feeling was intense, unending.

"Something's wrong," I panted as a wave of nausea struck out of nowhere. It felt like I was being torn apart from the inside out, but I was increasingly aware of a tightening in the center of my abdomen.

My hand went there, to the source of it all.

"Is it... is it the baby?" Beth asked.

I could only nod, confirming.

That *had* to be it.

Up until now, I barely even noticed I was carrying. Life was completely normal, even when I'd taken on the soldier a week ago.

But as I lay there, curled into myself hoping it brought me comfort, I was all too aware of the life inside me.

"Ok breathe, Evie," Beth urged, keeping her hand on my back as she got to her knees. "It ... it has to be that thing you were telling me about. The cresting or whatever it was, right? Isn't this when Elise said it would happen?"

I managed to focus long enough to go back to that moment, to think of what Elise had shared with me. She was clear that if I were to present as a dragon, the process would be far quicker than if I presented as a wolf. She described it as intense and, if nothing else, what I was feeling now was intense.

"I can't," I panted. "I can't do this."

"Yes, you can. You're a freakin' queen for Pete's sake, Evie. You've got this. *We've* got this," she amended, moving her palm from my back to take my hand. "Just breathe and I'll get some help."

Unable to think, I didn't give any input. All I knew was I wanted this, whatever it was, to be over.

"Help!" Beth called out. "Something's wrong! Can anybody hear me?"

I fell over on my side and the room blurred. There were words leaving my mouth in mumbled, half syllables, but I couldn't make sense of any of it.

"Help!" she called out again. "I can hear you out there! Please!"

She was quiet for a few seconds before crouching to the slit where our meals had come in. Part of me hoped someone came— although I had no clue what a horde of soldiers could or *would* do to help me. The other part of me hoped they ignored Beth's plea, fearing what they'd do when they found me like this. There'd been no compassion for us since arriving here, so I wouldn't expect them to have it now.

"I think someone's coming," Beth whispered, turning to listen again.

The burn subsided marginally, and I placed a hand on my stomach. When I did, I was startled to feel that it had swelled. The change was slight—so slight no one else would notice without touching that same spot—but this wasn't my imagination.

She held her breath when someone approached and backed away from the door when a folded sheet of paper was dropped into the slot.

No conversation.

No help.

Just another piece of paper that probably held *another* empty promise—just like the one we'd been given the night we arrived. The one who claimed they'd help us never made good on their word. If they had, we wouldn't still be in this mess.

Beth practically ripped it in half trying to open it, sighing as she read the message aloud.

'TOMORROW.'

I had no clue what, exactly, would happen tomorrow, but I was groggy and couldn't hold a coherent thought in my head. The one thing I *did* know was that, from here on out, my condition would progress a lot quicker.

While I felt nothing but terror for what the future held, I was certain this discovery would make *one* person very happy—Sebastian. He had some wicked plan for this baby, a plan I felt sick just imagining. If we were going to make it out of this situation alive, something would have to give. And soon.

There was only one I knew could save us and I called out to him in my thoughts despite knowing the message would never reach him.

'*Liam, wherever you are ... we need you.*'

CHAPTER 18

Liam

The more I thought about it, the more I believed a theory I formed within a few minutes of us leaving the house was true. Elise had purposely arranged for me to ride alone with her and Hilda as we trekked to Ridge Borough. She'd cloaked her intentions well, her invitation seeming innocent enough, but this was definitely a setup.

"You're certain everyone's clear on the plan?" Hilda asked, aiming her question at me. My guess was that their intentions were to talk so much I couldn't focus on the rage, thus keeping me levelheaded.

They definitely had the excessive talking part down.

I gave a nod. "Everyone knows what their jobs and positions are."

From the passenger seat beside Elise, Hilda returned the nod.

"Good. Tonight must be executed with razorlike precision. Even the slightest slipup could prove detrimental."

With that statement, she'd earned herself a stern look from Elise. I guessed she didn't approve of Hilda's remark.

She moved on after an expected eye roll.

"The witches are being removed from the premises as we speak. The sisterhood from Mogue Rock spent the entire night preparing. It's no small feat to dampen the power of an entire coven, and then entrance them to leave town in a single-file line," she said with a laugh, exaggerating that last part. Although, the process was pretty close.

The witches leaving in one massive wave would have sent up all kinds of red flags, alerting Sebastian of our intent to strike. So, instead, the spell would work subtly. They would leave in small groups of three, each one sensing and responding to an inexplicable call to head North, toward the edge of the woods. Once they arrived, they'd find a massive tribe of ancient magic wielders waiting to act as judge, jury and executioner. Their task was to identify the witch who cursed the weapons. Once she successfully undid the spell, she and all the others would be put to death.

Like they deserved.

"And the parameter is already sealed?" Elise asked next.

Hilda gave a dutiful nod. "Sealed and impenetrable."

"Speaking of," Elise chimed in again, "are we certain everyone's been marked? Because if they haven't, they won't be able to pass through the seal. We can't afford for anyone to—"

"No one will be left behind," Hilda interjected. "I oversaw the marking myself. In fact, I've still got henna on my fingers," she added as she peered down at the smudges.

At the mention of it, my eyes drifted down to the very mark they spoke of, placed on my inner-wrist just like the rest of our clan. To most, it would have looked like a tangle of random lines and shapes, but it was much more than that. Without it, we would be trapped in Ridge Borough at the stroke of midnight ... when the final act of our strategy would be carried out.

Around my neck, a handful of necklaces hung, each with the same symbol etched on it to allow the ones who wore them passage into the safe zone. There were enough for Evangeline, Beth, and one for the kid who worked for us from inside Sebastian's camp.

Elise breathed deep, gripping the steering wheel as our convoy headed toward our intended mark. We'd done our share of debating and planning. Now, the time had finally come to act.

And we were all beyond ready.

I hated that so much time had passed, but as I stood with my back to a tree, I closed my eyes and allowed myself to feel her, imagine I'd have her in my arms again soon. The only way I knew she was nearby was because intel had brought us here.

There was no definitive extraction point where I'd find Evangeline, because they needed to be able to move her on a whim, should a place come under heavy fire. So, there were just characteristics we agreed upon—the place would be moderate to small in size, would be at a higher elevation than most of the other structures, and we would find a red strip of fabric tied to the door knob. Other than that, we were heading in blind.

I tried not to dwell on the fact that I'd checked and re-checked this area daily since Evangeline had been taken. I had to keep the faith, had to believe we hadn't been led astray. If I thought about it too long, doubt would creep in and I'd start thinking this had all been for nothing. But I had to trust that we were in the right place.

Things were quiet, too quiet for this town to be the hideout for an entire lycan army. Still, this was where we were told we would find them.

"Is everything in place?" Dallas whispered into his radio,

waiting for the reply of a guard. Once he got confirmation, he gestured for us to move forward.

All of us—Elise, her boys, Hilda, Nick's brothers and friends.

No one stayed behind because this mission was too important. Twenty-four hours after being told with certainty that Evangeline was here, we had something we hadn't had since she left.

Leverage.

With so many loose ends to tie up, we had no choice but to bring in help. Had it not been for those willing to lend a hand, tonight's plan would only be another battle in a long-standing war.

But if all went according to plan, we would be closing the door on this chapter of our lives.

For good.

"How do we know they're not already waiting for us?" Lucas rambled, overflowing with nervous energy. "Or, better yet, how do we know they're not already surrounding us?"

"Man, I think you need to look up the meaning of the word *'better'*, cause what you just described ain't it," Chris sighed, following the rest of us as we headed into town.

We had a tight time limit to get in, get Evangeline and Beth, and get out. The deadline: midnight.

"We'll take the main road in," Dallas decided. "Doesn't make sense to go in quietly. Not with all the noise we intend to make in a few, right?"

I was in total support of his full-steam ahead approach. Whatever got us in and out the fastest. The streets looked abandoned, but that didn't mean anything. There were likely lycans watching us from the windows of the many abandoned warehouses and shops we passed. But we were getting nowhere.

"You sure this is the place?" Lucas asked, scanning the area.

"It is. Now pipe down," Dallas snapped.

He was far nicer than I would have been.

We stopped and took a moment to assess our odds.

"Gentlemen, I believe it's time we make ourselves known," Ethan chimed in, and at his words my heart raced just at the thought of finally ending this.

"Good enough for me," I said only to our team, speaking loudly the next second, addressing whatever enemies were close enough to hear.

"Show yourselves!" I called out, stopping in the middle of the street to see if any dared to come out of hiding. "Stop waiting for the Sovereign to give an order. Show yourselves and fight like men."

My voice echoed, being carried off in the wind.

Nothing.

No one responded or made a sound. They weren't budging because they didn't dare make a move without Sebastian telling them to do so.

When I reached for the duffle bag Dallas carried on his back, he eyed me curiously as I removed the large rifle. After checking to make sure it was loaded and ready to go, I clutched it, aiming for the vacant windows.

"What are you doing? This isn't in the plans," he reasoned.

I glanced down at my wrist, checking the time. The minutes were disappearing quicker than I cared to admit, and we all knew what would happen at midnight.

"Way I see it, there are only two ways to get them out here. One is for Sebastian to command it. The other is if we *force* them out," I explained. "Considering our deadline, I'm going with option B."

The next sound to be heard was that of bullets blasting out windows. I'd completely destroyed an entire floor of a hospital before stopping myself. The only reason I came to my senses was the realization that Evangeline and Beth could have been somewhere inside. Had it not been for that, I would have reloaded and fired until someone came out to play.

However, my soundcheck seemed to have finally gotten the attention of a few, because, all of a sudden, this was no longer a dress rehearsal ... the show was getting ready to begin.

"Stay out of trouble and stick to the plan," I said as a final warning to the team before we fanned out. And with a short whistle, our entire clan poured out into the open.

Sebastian brought this war on himself, and he was about to find out how hard I, and the others, were willing to fight for our queen.

I was either coming out of this *with* her ... or I wasn't coming out at all.

Evie

Something was going on out there. Not only could Beth and I *hear* it, but bright bursts of light, explosions, could also be seen from our small, barred window.

She stood on the tips of her toes to get a better look while I lie on the mattress. I'd learned to cope with the slight pain that lingered after last night's spike. I guessed it hadn't left completely because my stomach continued to grow while I got what little sleep I could. It still wasn't completely distended, but had rounded significantly.

So much so, Beth could now see the difference from the day before.

With the change, I was also aware that I no longer had the ability to shift, and probably wouldn't again until after the child was born. Speaking of ... there was something else that suddenly made this experience more real ... movement. I actually *felt* the baby now, which was way sooner than I imagined most women did. He or she bumped around in there every so often, surprising me every time.

I glanced around at the walls, wondering how, or even *if* I'd ever get out of here. This whole time, I'd been so afraid to embrace the idea of motherhood. The chaos we existed in had stolen that from me. And now, as I lie there staring down at the evidence of a love so powerful not even *time* could erase it … I wanted nothing more than to enjoy the experience. I had to hold on to the hope that, one day soon, I might get that chance—an opportunity to share this all with Liam.

My eyes shifted toward the window again as another loud blast just outside it rocked the entire building. I had to believe that was him, he'd come for me and … I don't know … maybe it was safe to start hoping now.

Maybe.

Beth moved away from the window and began to pace. She'd been so levelheaded this entire time, only now did I see her iron-clad bravery beginning to waver. It had never been our intent for her to fill the role as my *Keeper*, but based on what I'd been told about them, she fit the role to a tee. She was a warrior, one who'd dedicated herself to protecting me while I was unable to protect myself.

We were locked in here like animals and, with things quickly falling apart outside, it wouldn't take long for them to get worse in here, too.

"We need to move," she panted. In a fit of desperation, she rushed toward the door and slammed it with her foot, backing up to do the same again and again.

Not even a dent, but that didn't stop her from trying another few times before giving in.

"They can't keep us here like this," she breathed. "Someone has to—"

The words were stolen right from her mouth when a sound at the door had both our attention. A metal tinkering in the lock maybe made her heart race just like mine. With the creak of the hinges, the door we'd stared at for more than a week ... was finally open.

On the other side of it, our savior, the one who had only given us handwritten messages until now, promises we had no idea he intended to keep. A black, fitted mask covered most of his face, but his eyes ... they were so familiar. With the way Beth stared, I was certain she recognized him, too, but ...

"Errol ...?" Her voice was shrill. It wasn't until she said his name that I understood why he was so familiar.

During our stay at the Damascus Facility, he and Beth had gotten close, their budding interest in one another only being hindered by our abrupt extraction and return to our respective homes. Now, somehow, he was here.

Saving us.

"What are ... I don't understand," Beth rambled, reaching for my hand while she spoke, helping me to my feet.

I followed her back to the door where she stared into the eyes of the boy she'd only let go of because she had to.

"It's me," he panted, handing over what looked like two dark cloaks he expected us to put on. "We have to go," he urged, his nervous energy quickly transferring to us.

I slipped the rough material over my head without question and Beth did the same. The next second, she took his hand and mine and we were led from our cell.

Our pace was slow and incredibly cautious. At every corner we had to crouch behind Errol as he checked for guards, or worse yet, Sebastian and Blaise. I had the sense of this place crawling with lycans while we were held here, but now, with the fight that had been brought to them outside, I gathered that most had gone out to defend their newly claimed territory. When the coast was clear, he gestured for us to move forward.

The pain in my abdomen spiked with each step and it felt like my heart would leap from my chest. I wouldn't dare ask them to stop, though. Not when freedom was so close, not when our lives depended on it. My only option was to draw on the strength I knew I had inside and keep going.

We came to a narrow hallway and stopped when two deep voices echoed off the walls. Errol extended his hand, silently instructing us to duck down again before he peeked from around the corner to check. Only, when he did, one of the guards spotted him and a loudly spoken, "Run!" sent Beth and I scurrying for the open door we passed a few feet back.

She slammed and locked it behind us. It was a tightly confined supply closet, but it was also the only thing shielding us from whoever Errol scuffled with on the other side.

Beth's face was riddled with concern. I knew that, had it not been for my condition, she would have stayed with him and fought. However, her extreme loyalty had her standing not by my side, but in front of me like the protector she was as we huddled in a corner listening.

Listening and waiting.

The hallway went quiet and we didn't move an inch. I even held my breath as I stared at the door when someone approached, hoping and praying it would be—

"Errol!" Beth gasped, only letting go of my hand when she couldn't help herself, when she rushed toward him and threw her arms around his neck.

He embraced her tightly as he panted from the altercation.

"I told you I'd get you out of here," he said, his words being spoken into Beth's hair as they clung to one another. "But we have to move. More guards will come and I have strict orders to get you all someplace safe for extraction."

"Whose orders?" I asked quietly, following him and Beth from the closet we hid in.

Errol kept his eyes trained straight ahead as he shrugged. "There's an entire network," he explained. "All I know is I take orders from the people who planted me here. No clue who calls the shots for them, though."

We stopped and crouched again when a large door came into view. It was across a wide-open common area I felt incredibly uneasy about crossing. Granted, it looked like we were alone here, but I wasn't so sure. If someone popped up while we were making a run for it ...

"Let's move," Errol instructed, being careful to stick close to the wall to minimize exposure. Still, I was sweating bullets.

With a hard shove he flung the door open and I breathed deep, taking in fresh air for the first time in over a week. I had no clue where we were headed from here, but *anything* was better than where we'd been—stuck in a dark, musty prison, knowing our days were numbered.

"Go, go go!" Errol urged, commanding us to run ahead of him where we could hide behind an old shed on the property. He checked for eyes again and then rushed across the yard to where we waited.

"Where are you leading us?" Beth asked, taking the words right out of my mouth.

Panting and keeping watch, Errol smiled a little.

"Well, I was told to take you all someplace high up, someplace I least expected Sebastian to find you. So, I figured what better place to hide you from a devil ... than a church."

Beth and I followed his gaze as bullets and explosions accompanied the screams and earthshattering growls that surrounded us. Our eyes locked on the small, white building at the top of a hill.

This was it. We reached the end of our journey and, from here, we'd know whether we won this fight or lost it.

As the little one inside tumbled around, making my will to survive that much stronger, I had to hope for the best.

CHAPTER 19

Nick

Outside was a warzone.

Everything we anticipated, our worst fears, were manifesting right before our eyes. My own included.

My wrists ached where the chains had cut into them for days, and every other part of my body matched the pain. This—being locked away and forced into being sired by Sebastian—had been a living hell.

With nothing in my system other than his blood, I felt oddly powerful despite not being fed. When they took notice of the shift from being weak and disoriented to alert and showing signs of increased strength, they were quick to reinforce the chains with thicker ones that would do a better job of holding me here.

I hung there, staring at the covered windows that surrounded me. Breathing deep, my nostrils flared as I let my eyes close, feeling my veins swell with darkness. In the time I'd spent here, I wasn't sure if it was that I now had Sebastian's wickedness swirling around inside my head, but ... I no longer felt the dual need to kill and save Evie. Only one inclination remained. I didn't care that she once meant something to me, didn't care that her life meant something to so many. I only wanted her dead.

My next thought was of Roz, how she'd feel if she saw me now, if she were to see what I'd become. Being near her had made it easier to fight what I really was, made it easier to be a better man.

Now, I didn't even consider myself a person. I was something completely different.

Something that lived, breathed, and thrived on darkness.

Slow footsteps approached from behind and I didn't bother trying to maneuver my body that way to see who'd come. I *knew* who'd come, could feel his life source coursing through my veins like it was my own.

"We've reached a crucial point in our time together, Nicholas," Sebastian sighed. "It's been brought to my attention that our *other* guests have been ... released without consent," he shared. "And I'm certain you're aware of why I can't have that."

Even before he'd come in with the update, I knew Evie had gone, because I felt her. My sense of her had gotten so keen in the passing days, I knew exactly how many yards separated us. Knew exactly how many steps I'd have to take to get to her.

Sebastian circled me once before coming to a stop at my feet. He scanned me, his eyes tracing the dark veins that lined muscle—muscle that had swelled to nearly twice it's size with the transformation. At the sight of my new appearance, a pleased, wicked grin parted his thin lips.

"I haven't come around to visit in a day or two, and it looks like you've ... come into your own," he remarked.

The very next second, he gestured for a guard to approach.

"Keys," he stated, holding his hand out expectantly.

The guard's gaze rose to meet mine and I noted the fact that he didn't seem as sure of this as Sebastian did. However, he had no choice but to obey.

I focused on the glint of metal in his palm, watching as he took it upon himself to release the chains that weighed down my ankles. The prospect of being released had my heart racing double time.

Sebastian leveled a glare as he gestured for a second guard to lower me from the rafter I'd been strung from since I first arrived.

A mechanical whirring filled the room and my chest heaved with relief the second my feet were flat on the ground. The chains around my wrists rattled when my arms lowered, no longer stretching the sore tendons beneath them.

I had Sebastian's full attention as he stared through me. I guessed he was only hesitant because, with me being different, he couldn't be certain the sire bond had taken completely.

I didn't move, just stood in place as he observed, and eventually used that same key to undo the chains on my wrists. Again, the pleased smile twisted his otherwise darkened expression.

"Well ... I suppose we can consider our little experiment a success," he announced, his deep voice reverberating off the walls.

The few guards who stood watch around the room were still visibly skeptical—maybe because a few had taken advantage of my immobility and used excessive force just for kicks and giggles. Now that I was free, they seemed unsure of what my next move would be.

"How do you feel?" Sebastian asked.

A question to which there was only one answer. "Never better."

"That's what I love to hear," he said approvingly, backing away before testing the next leg of this process. One I enjoyed based purely on the sheer terror it brought his guards when he uttered one word.

"... Kill."

A deep roar forced its way from my lungs. I was instantly on one of Sebastian's men, feeling the resistance of his flesh beneath my claws just before the satisfying tear as they first pierced his arms, then his legs ... his eyes. Once he was effectively pinned and defenseless, I bit down on his neck. The taste of his blood only made me stronger, more ferocious. I locked my teeth around an artery and ripped it free, causing blood to spurt from the gaping wound and onto the floor and wall.

This, the killing was ... satisfying.

"Enough," Sebastian called out, prompting my entire body to freeze other than my heaving chest and shoulders. "That was all I needed to see. You've convinced me of your loyalty."

I stood to my feet, covered in the slick blood of the lycan I attacked.

Sebastian approached, looking me over with pride behind his gaze. "You're ready for phase three," he said, holding my attention. "I tried to keep the hybrid alive, but she's proven time and time again that she will never cooperate. So, it is with regret for what could have been, that I have to send you out into the world to do what it is you were born to do."

Excitement rose within me, anticipating what his next charge would be.

"Bring her to me," he ordered. "Dead or alive."

Evie

"I think we should run for it," Beth spoke up.

Her head popped up from behind the pew, covered by what, after a week without brushing, was now a blonde nest. Her skin and hair took on the oddly spaced red, blue and green geometric shapes of the stained-glass windows surrounding us. Beneath our knees where we crouched, the torn pages from the congregation's hymnals and debris from years of abandonment, looters, and stray animals.

"What if we were supposed to go further out?" she asked next. "Someplace further away. Someplace outside this godforsaken town."

Errol didn't budge as he shook his head. "We can't risk moving again. They'll find us. I put the red strip on the knob like they said to do, so ... they'll find us," he repeated.

While I, too, felt a bit vulnerable here, I agreed with Errol's logic. I was certain that, if we left again, we might not be as lucky as when we fled from the prison.

"We'll just ... wait here, and someone will come," was Errol's attempt at a comforting word.

So, for now, we were basically stuck here, but at least we had each other.

"Got food on you by any chance?" Beth asked. When prompted, Errol proceeded to dig into the pocket of the dark hoodie he wore. My eyes lit up with hope he'd come out with something good, but it was only gum—one measly stick at that.

It disappeared from his fingers and was split between us before he could even offer it. We hadn't eaten since the day before and even when the guards *did* feed us, it was mostly table scraps from their own meals. So, yeah, a stick of gum was like a buffet to us at the moment.

We were plunged into silence, hearing only the commotion that went on outside and our own light scuffling over the mess that covered the floor. I was just going to see what other info Errol had to share when Beth spoke up instead.

"So ... you're kind of like a spy, huh?"

Errol glanced at her and nodded. "I guess you could say that."

"Impressive," Beth added with a smile, and there was no missing the redness that tinted Errol's entire face when she did.

"It beat having to return to my hometown, pretending like being at Damascus didn't change my life," he replied. "I know we didn't get to stay for the full experience, but it still impacted me in a big way."

"Big enough for you to risk your life saving us tonight," Beth observed.

This time, Errol was slow to speak, keeping his eyes trained on her.

"Yeah ... I guess you could say that."

These two were so much alike—competitive, fearless, loyal. Heck, he hadn't seen Beth in months, but he still thought nothing of coming to our aid tonight.

"So ... when whoever you take orders from told you to help us, did you know who we were?" she asked next.

Errol smiled a bit. In my opinion, there were very few things that could make a guy smile at a girl in a situation like this. He had to have some pretty intense feelings for her, which I suspected to be true.

"I uh ... I saw you the day the soldiers brought you two in. Your eyes were covered, so it took me a sec to convince myself I wasn't seeing things, but ... then I knew," he shared. "Actually, even before orders came down, I was already working on a plan to break you guys free. But let's just say I was incredibly grateful when I got the order and realized I wouldn't be on my own. Having an entire army behind you makes things a bit easier."

Beth smiled at that. "Well, I'm glad it was you."

I smiled, too, watching them dance around their feelings, still too focused on the mission to own them. The most I could do was hope they'd get a chance to explore them once this all blew over.

The sweet moment between them was shattered into a million pieces when a soul-crushing roar filtered beneath the door, through the walls themselves. It didn't sound like any of the others that had torn through the area tonight. It was ... different.

"What the heck was that?" Errol asked, his eyes widening when he seemed to reach the same conclusion I had. Whatever made that noise wasn't your average, everyday shifter.

I swallowed hard as a thought passed through my head. I was quickly reminded of a lycan. One who was *far* from ordinary.

"I think ... I ... that's ... that has to be Nick," I stammered, hating how prevalent the presence of terror was in my voice. "Sebastian must have set him free."

For a time, Sebastian seemed hellbent on laying claim to the child I carried. He must have changed his mind about how much trouble I was worth or maybe even thought he'd just use Nick to find me and bring me out of hiding. Only, if that was the case, he'd grossly underestimated the hold this curse had on Nick.

Because, if he found me, he'd kill me.

"We have to hide her someplace else," Beth said in a rush. "Someplace safer than this. He'll hear her heartbeat and then come straight for her."

Errol stood, not bothering to ask questions as he took Beth's hand and practically sprinted from our hiding spot between the pews.

"There's an attic," he panted. "I came to check this place out a few nights ago and found a way up there. The main stairs have rotted and caved, but there's a ladder we can use to bridge the gap, and then pull it up with us so no one suspects anyone's crossed it."

He didn't understand.

There was no outsmarting Nick, no hiding in an attic and hoping for the best. Beth and I shared a glance and I believed we shared the same thought as well.

The only chance we had ... was to run for it.

"We might be able to get out in front of him if we stick to the woods," I suggested, pulling the hood of the cloak over my head.

"But, Evie," Beth interjected, her gaze drifting down toward my stomach where, just beneath the loose-fitting material, my newly-rounded stomach ached and burned with the sudden growth, but ... we had no choice.

"I'll be fine," I lied, knowing the pain I felt would only increase if I overdid it, but I was certain death would be worse.

We moved toward the door and it wasn't until Beth stared at me with that hopeless look that I realized I had teared up. The next second, a few fell and there was no hiding it. We didn't have time for our emotions to get in the way, though. The proof of this was the sound of another of those bloodcurdling roars.

And he was closer.

"Promise me something," I sniffled, doing what I could to conceal how distraught I was on the inside. "Promise me that, no matter what, you won't look back," I said. "Promise me you won't slow down or double back because of me."

Beth was already shaking her head before I even finished. "Absolutely not," she rebutted. "We're in this together, Evie. I'm not leaving you."

She was making this so, *so* hard.

"It's not you he wants," I went on. "I can't be responsible for anything happening to you. Your family needs you and I'm the one who got us into this mess."

That part of my statement confused her, but it was true.

"If I hadn't chased down the soldier. If I hadn't—"

"You did what was right," she cut in. "You went after that soldier because you have more heart than anyone else I know. You went after him because ... you're a born leader, Evie. And the good ones are strong and selfless. Just like you."

I didn't know what to say. I'd done my best to offer her an honest, no-strings-attached, guilt-free way out of this, but ...

"Either we make a move together, or we don't move at all," was Beth's final thought.

She took my hand and we made the decision to step out into the night as a team. Errol opened the front door of the church and our hearts were prepared to face the night. However, as I stared out, a set of huge, yellow eyes heading straight up the hill for us meant our plan had just changed.

None of us would be going anywhere.

CHAPTER 20

Liam

My hair and skin were soaked with blood, and the mutts were still coming at us fast and hard. Dallas, Elise, and half her boys had taken to the air, slaying Sebastian's dragon recruits. Declan and Ethan stayed grounded to beat back the wave of mutts and soldiers. There were so many, and all I could think about was how each one stood between me and Evangeline.

She was somewhere out there—alive but not safe.

With the anarchy that erupted here in Ridge Borough, she had to have been terrified. I couldn't imagine what this time in captivity had been like for her. It was of little comfort imagining how I'd make Sebastian pay for what he'd done.

But I did pray that I'd be the one to end him.

I was owed at least that.

Richie and both his brothers were keeping up with the number of lives Declan, Ethan, and I had reached. For every life *we* took, each of them had taken one as well. I'd foregone the use of a weapon and resorted to doing what felt natural—fighting with my bare hands. Even though my veins glowed red, I continued to suppress the flames. Burning the bastards to death was too good for them. Today these cowards would die the good old-fashioned way.

I killed for Evie. I killed for Ivan who still suffered. I killed for Elise who, like me, had lost everything once. I killed for Noah's legacy to thrive like it was always meant to. I killed so our family could live in peace—something we never had a chance at before. When my limbs became fatigued, these were the thoughts that kept me going.

Roz, Lucas, and Chris caught up, and from the looks of them, they'd taken on just as many as we had. Wounds and gashes on their arms, legs, and torsos told of a few close calls, but they were still on their feet, fighting.

"Behind you!" Roz called out, but I was already on it. The mutt that attempted to use the element of surprise was met with an elbow to the throat. Stunned, he didn't even put up a fight when I palmed his face, smashing the back of his head to mush against a tree.

We were making a bit of progress, but we didn't intend to take this army out one by one. We had a bigger plan, one that would sweep the entire area clean, but that couldn't begin until I had Evangeline and Beth in my possession.

In between being attacked by mutts and soldiers, I scanned the area, looking for where she might have been and ... that's when I heard it, a guttural howl that made the hairs on the back of my neck stand on end.

I'd heard the sound before—the morning Nick showed up at our door doing all he could to claw his way to Evangeline. I'd heard it centuries ago as I chased his predecessor into the night.

"He's loose," I yelled, signaling the rest of the team.

They made quick work of finishing their current fight and then moved in closer to form a tight unit. We *all* had reason to track Nick down. His brothers and Roz hoped to wrangle him in before midnight, still clinging to a hope that he could be saved, but my one and only goal was to retrieve Evangeline and Beth. As far as Nick was concerned, I saw this ending one way and one way only for him.

We moved out quickly to outrun what would come next.

"North," Caleb called out, raising his voice over the noise.

Above, Dallas and Elise dropped in altitude, following as we pressed forward.

"I ... I think I see something."

I glanced at Chris after he spoke, following his gaze to where they focused up ahead. And, sure enough, I spotted a dark shadow. My initial thought was that this was just another lycan, but ... then I realized I was wrong.

What I stared at was massive, a killing machine in the flesh, and he was tearing his way up a steep hill, trying to get to something.

Or someone.

At the top of that hill sat a small, white church—it's stained-glass windows and silhouetted steeple standing out in the moon-light. He was getting close, but there was still time to stop him. At least ... that's what I kept telling myself.

With how he barreled toward the mark, I was positive Evangeline had to be inside.

Now, I only needed to get to her before he did.

I couldn't afford to fail or let anything stand in my way, but as if the universe heard and responded to my thoughts ...

Two foreboding figures emerged from the thick fog that had fallen. Both walked with the slow gait of self-important royalty, carrying with them an air that implied they were invincible. Only, if I had anything to do with it, they would soon be convinced otherwise.

"This is quite the show you've put on," Sebastian remarked, gesturing further down the hillside where his army and the Seaton Falls clan collided in battle. "After more than a week, I actually thought we might have been rid of you for good this time, but you've always been a resilient one, Reaper. Which is more than I think we can say for your mate."

My fists clenched at my sides and adrenaline pumped through my veins. At his words, I gazed uphill to where the church sat off in the distance. I no longer heard or saw Nick, but was certain he was still stalking about.

"Speaking of your mate," Sebastian spoke up again, "we were pleased to see her dragon present, which *would* have made for a speedy gestation. However, as I'm sure you're already aware, our friend the Liberator seems to be on the loose, so we all know how that will end."

"Again," Blaise added, keeping his eyes trained on me as he waited for a reaction.

He and Sebastian shared a dark laugh. At the sound of it, I felt the heightened energy of our team all around me, each one waiting for my signal to launch an attack. Sebastian had given them more than enough reasons to. However, we had to be smart. Sebastian's army could not be seen, but I sensed them lurking. Glancing up into the trees, dark silhouettes shifted, confirming my suspicion.

"I've waited entirely too long to send you back to hell where you belong, but I plan on fixing that today." I felt my chest and shoulders heave as the unquenchable longing to make good on this promise overpowered me.

A slow, sinister smile turned the corners of Sebastian's mouth upward. "You sound like a man prepared to kill or be killed," he laughed. "I suppose that's fitting ... seeing as how the Liberator is likely already sucking remnants of your beloved from his teeth."

Rage swelled inside me and the edges of my vision darkened like a tunnel, staying intently focused on Sebastian. Bright red flames ignited, bursting from my hands and quickly spreading until my entire body was ablaze. The added strength and ferocity that came along with being turned surged like a flood.

Sebastian shifted partially, but still mostly had the appearance of the man he pretended to be. He never looked away as he came straight for me, unsheathing a long blade from the holster at his hip. The flawless metal glinted in the moonlight as our long-standing feud was about to come to an end.

This was not a battle he'd be content to stand by and watch his soldiers fight, because our feud was personal. He'd taken so much from me over the centuries, and I'd evaded death by his hand more times than I could count. For me, this was about avenging Evangeline. For him, it was about settling a score.

The tip of his blade narrowly missed my throat when he swung it. He was wise not to get too close, knowing if I had the chance to set him on fire, it would end him. He wielded it through the air for a second time, passing it through the smoke billowing from the right side of my body.

My hands felt strange and I peered down at them. The flames at their centers moved wildly and, right before my eyes, they stretched and twirled in strange ways. Within seconds two objects, one in each hand, began to take shape.

They were ... weapons.

A large axe in one, a thick sword in the other.

Sebastian stared, his eyes alight with intrigue—his penchant for anomalies among supernaturals still present even now.

I didn't have time to think or rationalize, just act. I swung the axe toward Sebastian, feeling the weight of it in my hand, as if it was a tangible object I held. I swung again and, this time, I managed to knock his blade away. His gaze followed as it tumbled across the ground. He was unarmed, but far from defenseless.

Time was running out, so I acted quickly to end this fight sooner rather than later. Around me, the team did the same, cutting down soldier after soldier, Declan choosing to take on Blaise.

I glanced toward the church again and Sebastian didn't waste time trying to get under my skin.

"You're already too late," he taunted, causing my heart to race as I wondered if he was right about that. "And do you know why?" he asked. "Because I always win. Don't you understand? Since the beginning of time, I've ruled these lands. And long after Evangeline's blood has soaked into the soil, I will *still* rule," his voice boomed.

I stared at my hands, the weapons outlined in flames, and wanted nothing more than for these moments to be Sebastian's last. Only, mere weapons weren't good enough. I wanted him to die in unspeakable pain, just like the endless suffering *I'd* lived through.

Heat rose from my lungs, and finally ripped from my throat in one thunderous explosion as I breathed red flames several feet in front of me. They fanned outward, first singeing the bark of the two trees beside me, then two lycans who meant to take me down before hitting my intended target.

Sebastian.

His eyes stretched wide with surprise when the first wave of heat touched his skin. And then, every tree within a mile must have quaked with the roar he released. It was the sound of several century's worth of evading defeat coming to an end.

Still on his feet, he tore at his flesh as if he'd somehow peel away the rapidly spreading fire.

The tantrum had finally garnered Blaise's attention, and the look of horror that spread across his face was almost as sweet as the one that had been on his father's. All it took was that one moment of distraction to give Declan the advantage he'd been fighting for and, in an instant, his broad wings sprang forth and with the sharp edge of one, he opened Blaise's throat. The poetic justice of this moment wasn't lost on me, remembering how I'd nearly ended him the same way a short time ago.

He staggered back, clutching the wound. Within seconds, he picked up speed and I knew his plan. He intended to get away, hiding in the shadows until he healed and could avenge his father. However, I wasn't the only one who noticed his attempt to escape. Before he got too far out, Ethan dashed toward him and wasted no time. He placed one hand on Blaise's chin, and with one quick snap, ripped his head right off his neck.

As Sebastian burned and sank to his knees, his eyes were trained on his son. I wondered what went through his mind, if he felt some inkling of remorse for letting his greed rob them both of a full life. I wondered if he thought of how simple it would have been to share the title of royalty with another original family, realizing it wouldn't have diminished his right in the least. Or maybe ... he only regretted not being one step ahead of me.

He eventually slumped against a tree for support, but I promptly shoved him onto his back using the sole of my boot. His eyes were then fixed above on the stars, but he didn't deserve even an *ounce* of peace in death. So, I stood over him and made sure the only emotion he felt as his final breath hissed from between his lips was hatred.

His for me.

Mine for him.

Elise swooped down, the body of a now-deceased dragon hitting the ground seconds before she did. She was winded, but alert as she approached, seeing what was left of Sebastian, Blaise.

Her hand pressed to my shoulder and I was pleased to hear that our priorities were still aligned.

"We'll deal with the rest and follow you when we can."

I nodded, glancing toward where we last heard Nick. I took

one step and with four words, Elise let down her guard and exposed her heart.

"Liam ... save our girl."

I walked away knowing she was well aware that I'd do whatever it took to make that come to pass.

CHAPTER 21

Evie

I
t was Nick, but ... he'd changed. His arms and neck had swelled, doubled in size as thick, black veins covered him completely. He hadn't even shifted into his wolf—covered in the telltale silver fur—but there was no questioning whether he had fully succumbed to the curse of the Liberator.

We, officially, had no place else to run.

Blinking as Nick stared past Beth and Errol, directly at me, I took a step back. As soon as I did, my stomach rolled with movement, a small body inside my own reacting to the terror I felt, the stress of seeing Nick like this.

He'd been such a good friend when I moved to Seaton Falls. Eventually, more than that, before the dust settled and I realized with whom my heart truly belonged. But now, as he crossed the threshold with murderous thoughts and hatred in his eyes, I imagined I was the only one who remembered any of those things. To him, I was now nothing more than a target.

"You two have to get out of here," I urged, going back to my original stance, one that wouldn't require Beth—a loved one—to perish because of me.

She ignored me, though, keeping an arm stretched in front of my chest, being the protector she always said she'd be. Errol held his ground right beside Beth, their bodies blocking me from Nick, like human shields.

"Nick ... don't do this," Beth pleaded, still managing to sound fearless as she all but begged her friend to resist his nature.

But he didn't listen. Instead, he took another step, closing the distance between us.

I heard the faint rumble of Beth's wolf from deep within. It was responding to the threat Nick posed and I imagined, had I not yet crested, mine would have done the same.

There was a silent standoff as we watched, waited. I held out hope that Nick would be able to fight this, but when he lunged in our direction ... that hope ... it evaporated in the wind.

His mass, formidable as it was, collided with Beth's. She'd shifted in the blink of an eye and met Nick in the air. Fabric from her clothes, the cloak she'd worn to conceal her identity, tore and fluttered gently to the ground. The sight of the material falling so gracefully was a stark contrast to the violence that erupted right after. Errol didn't have time to think. He, instead, acted on instinct, leaping to Beth's rescue.

Despite my condition, I barely even thought about myself, doing what I could to stop Nick, watching as his razor-sharp claws tore through Beth's flesh like wet paper. She yelped in pain and I could hardly see through the blur of tears that welled in my eyes, watching her fall victim to his strength. I managed to grab hold of one of his arms, hoping it'd be enough to pull him away from her, hoping even to distract him by dangling the one thing he wanted most in this life right before his eyes.

Me.

My life.

At first, I believed my plan worked, but then, when I was swatted away like a ragdoll, I realized it hadn't been enough. My body flew through the air until a large pillar stopped me in midair, my back slamming against it with a deafening crash.

Dazed, I struggled to get my bearings, but instead could only watch in horror as Nick raised one massive claw toward the ceiling. In a fleeting moment that seemed to pass in slow motion, he brought that claw down with swift precision ... tearing right through Beth's abdomen.

Breathless ... I stared.

This couldn't be happening.

She could not die here, not like this.

Not at all.

She cried out in pain and the sound of it struck bone, hitting me in the deepest parts of my soul. Errol's gaze shifted to meet mine and the shock behind it was mutual. It wasn't until she was injured that it set in how helpless the three of us were, how vulnerable. Feeling desperate and out of options, I did the one thing still in my power to save them.

"Get her out of here!" I yelled those words from the top of my lungs, praying Errol didn't try to be a hero. My fate was practically sealed, but I had to hope that, if he moved fast enough, that didn't have to be true for Beth.

"Take her as far away from Ridge Borough as you can and get her help," I added.

I knew what I was asking him to do. Essentially, if he listened, I'd be left here to fend for myself.

To face my demons alone.

Errol was only frozen for a moment, paralyzed by the sight of what had been done to Beth—her unconscious body completely still, blood beginning to seep from the corner of her mouth as she shifted back to human form. Things didn't look good and I had to force my tears into submission. I'd fought this as long as I could, and I had to be at peace with how it would end. We'd done everything we could.

Our fight to change the future had all been in vain.

Errol scrambled to cover Beth with the torn cloak beside her, lifting her from the floor before Nick could turn his attention from me to them, possibly thwarting their escape. He held her to his chest and I breathed deep with relief. I had to hope for the best, because *she* was the best. The best friend, best *sister*, a girl could ever hope for.

"Go!" I choked out.

Before rushing off, Errol passed a sympathetic glance in my direction, and then, in the blink of an eye, it was just us.

Me ... and Nick.

There was no place else to run. He was faster than me, especially now, so I didn't stand a chance. As I accepted this as my reality, my *fate*, I didn't think about myself. I thought only of those my death would cause pain—Elise, my brothers, Hilda, Liam.

Especially him.

It had broken him before. Losing me again would be soul-crushing, even more so the second time around. My only comfort was knowing he wouldn't be alone. He'd have my family surrounding him, helping him cope with the loss.

Both losses—me, our child.

I moved away from the beam I'd been thrown against, keeping my eyes trained on Nick's feet as he came closer, his heavy steps causing the old floorboards to creak and groan beneath his weight. I wished I hadn't noticed how intently his gaze was focused on not just me, but my stomach, as if the sound of the baby's heartbeat beckoned to him.

Swallowing hard, I felt the wetness in the corner of my eyes beginning to run down my cheeks. While I saw what Nick had become on the outside, I still hadn't forgotten who he'd been to me before—my savior on more than one occasion, my help when Sebastian took Liam and I had to go after him.

But he'd only been *any* of those things because of one defining characteristic.

He was a friend.

A good one.

Power swelled in his legs when he hunched toward the ground, and then thrust off his haunches in one seamless motion. He shifted from man to beast in midair, making it clear he intended to take me down when he landed. I closed my eyes, knowing how this would end, and just let go.

I stopped expecting a different outcome, stopped thinking I'd beat this and just ... found peace.

My body slammed the ground with such force I gasped for air. He held me down, heat from his breath sweeping the side of my face when I turned away. I couldn't look at him while he was like this.

Those sharp claws of his sank deep into my arms as he kept me pinned, inhaling the scent of my neck when he lowered, evaluating his prey. That's exactly what I was, his prey.

His victim.

In my last moments before it would all end, a wave of peace washed over me and my thoughts ... they became so clear. It was in the midst of this moment of extreme clarity that I spoke from my heart, because there wouldn't be another chance.

This was it.

"I forgive you, Nick," I sobbed, letting that statement roll off my quivering lips.

It was all I could do—a final gift for my friend locked away inside. I hoped that, once the deed was complete, once he was himself again and had to live with what he'd done, he'd remember this moment and would know I held no ill feelings toward him. Only the love of a friend. He couldn't help what he'd become, what this curse had turned him into, and I understood that.

The words seemed to go unnoticed. The proof of this was in his actions, as he raised his claws into the air again and brought it down, slicing through my cloak, tearing my skin with shallow gashes.

When the material fell away, he stared. The now tight-fitting tee I wore stretched across my stomach, revealing the roundness that hadn't been there a short time ago, not before the cresting. My pulse vibrated at the base of my neck and if I could have helped it I would have, knowing the sound of it likely pushed him toward the brink of insanity. It couldn't be helped though, not as my mind flooded with thoughts of him snuffing out the light of the budding life inside me.

My eyes closed, and it felt like the weight of the world fell on me, forcing out more tears as I lie beneath him. I hadn't even had the chance to fully embrace the idea of motherhood, but still, I was oddly aware of the growing bond between us—this small bundle I'd never get to hold.

I sometimes had a hard time grasping the concept of who I was, had a hard time accepting that I wasn't quite a teenager like I previously believed. In another life, I probably would have embraced this experience openly, but as I considered the loss ... the reality of it broke me, brought me to tears.

Nick stretched his hand and I waited ... waited for him to strike, waited for him to tear right through me, but ...

The sound of labored breathing that came next was not my own.

It was his.

My chest heaved as anticipation, confusion, and fear all over-powered me. Despite myself, I dared to open my eyes again, staring up as he gazed down, those piercing yellow eyes boring through me, but ... there was awareness in them. As in, the *real* him, for one fleeting moment, seemed to be present. I had no idea how or why, but ... it was him.

"Nick ..."

His brow creased with frustration when he turned away from the sound of his name. Right after, his weight shifted. It had once pinned me to the ground, but was suddenly lighter. Light enough that I was able to free my arms. When he didn't stop me, I quickly scooted away. Only a few inches at first, but then a few feet, bracing my back against the nearby pillar.

"Nick, if you can hear me ... fight it," I begged. "You're stronger than this."

His large shoulders heaved with each labored breath, but he didn't speak, didn't acknowledge that he comprehended my plea.

Warm air breezed over my lip as I kept a close eye on him, unsure of what he'd do next, unsure of what had even stopped him. His gaze lowered, and I was trapped in his stare. I felt my eyes stretch wider when, to my surprise, his wolf further submitted to the man. The silvery fur that covered him from head to toe shortened and thinned, eventually revealing the skin beneath. Thick, swollen muscle shrank to near-normal size, and sharp canines receded. Those dark veins that signified the curse were still visible, but he was more himself than monster.

Naked, he retreated into a dark corner and I wasn't sure what to think, what to do. So, I tried speaking again.

"Let me help you, Nick. I—"

"Kill me!"

A jolt shot through me when the harshly spoken words rang out in an unfamiliar voice. The statement burst from his lungs and ricocheted off the walls of the church, reverberating back to me like sound waves from a mighty bell.

When I didn't react quickly enough, he growled a second command, even more gruffly than the first time.

"Now, Evie! While you can, while I can control it!"

I no longer had a visual on him, but knew he had one on me as he fought this, as my heart raced a thousand miles an hour trying to process those words.

A request that had officially rendered me speechless.

"I—"

"Kill me!" he roared, the sound carrying with it and air of authority.

I sat straighter, unsure of what to do next. Instinct told me to run, but wisdom told me he'd only chase me and wouldn't stop until he succeeded. I could, literally, feel that I was slower, weaker now, as I guessed much of my strength went to the rapid growth of the baby.

Even if my heart would have let me do what he asked, it would take me shifting to one of my other forms and ... I couldn't.

"I can't hold it off much longer," he confessed, and I heard how much admitting that grieved him. "Grab something. Something sharp and, when I come at you, just make sure it goes through me."

I blinked away tears as that visual hit me like a ton of bricks.

"There has to be something else," I sobbed.

"There isn't," he said sternly, forcing my *own* emotions in check. "You're gonna do this because—"

His words cut off abruptly when a pained groan bellowed from his mouth. He gathered himself and forced the rest of the statement from his mouth.

"You're gonna do this because they need you. The clan, your family. I can't be the one to take you from them for a second time."

When he finished speaking, he struggled for breath.

This should have been an easy thing, choosing to put my own life ahead of his, but it wasn't. It was actually the hardest decision I ever had to make. If it hadn't been for the gentle flutter in my stomach reminding me I wasn't fighting for *me*, I might not have chosen to fight at all.

I might not have chosen life at the expense of someone else's.

I scanned my surroundings quickly for something to defend myself with, something sharp like Nick said to. The only thing I could get my hands on with so little time was a loose floorboard beside me. I tore it free, positioning myself just as a deafening roar shook the very foundation of the building. I settled one end of the makeshift weapon against the ground for leverage and I braced myself against the pillar.

In one final show of power, my dragon broke through. I felt her energy as I watched Nick leap toward me from the shadows, unable to fight his nature any longer. The brilliant blue flame that shot from the center of my palm ignited the entire board within the fraction of a second. I held it tight, keeping the sharp, ragged edge aimed outward.

It had come down to two choices. Only one of us could walk away from this alive and I couldn't be the one to decide. But because he was good to the core, Nick made the choice himself.

He chose me.

As I lifted the board higher into the air like he said to do, I closed my eyes and would keep them that way until it was over. A powerful impact was accompanied by a horrific sound, that of flesh being torn open, ribs being broken.

The force jarred my arm back, shoving my shoulder out of place and I cried out in pain, but the sound of my voice was the only sound in the entire building. A thick, deafening silence made my skin crawl with what it signified.

Death.

A heaviness peeled away from my soul, like a life-draining parasite had suddenly released me. I knew right away it was the feel of the curse being lifted. Tears rushed down my cheeks and ... I couldn't look at him, couldn't make myself see Nick like this.

His body and the plank both fell to the ground with a thud. Air sputtered from his mouth and my throat squeezed with emotion. There were so many bombarding me, like huge waves that came so fast I couldn't catch my breath before another was on top of me, pushing me under.

Somehow, he was still alive, although I knew it was only a matter of time until that changed. I forced my eyes open, finally taking in the sight of him, because this wasn't about me and what I was comfortable with. This was about comforting a friend through what little time he had left. I chose to only look into his eyes, not at the board protruding from his chest, not at the blue flames that were beginning to spread over his skin.

"I've got you," I promised as he groaned. "I'm not going anywhere."

I moved closer to settle at his side, clasping his hand in mine. My heart ached as the flames moved to his arms and neck, consuming him. The pain was nearly unbearable as he clenched my hand.

As tears fell, my mind went back to all the times he'd shown me what kindness was, how he'd accepted me into his circle, his life, when he could have easily shut me out. He'd opened himself to me without hesitation because he was good, right down to the core.

More wetness touched my cheeks and I knew I'd never forget the feel of his hand going limp in mine, the flames finally consuming him. I didn't let go. Couldn't even when it became clear it was over.

Just like that, eighteen years of life came to an end.

I released his hand, letting him rest in peace, vowing to never *ever* forget him, his sacrifice. Even with his last breath, he'd been selfless.

There were footsteps, and then ...

"Evangeline?"

In the midst of despair and brokenness, that voice caused both, my head *and* my heart, to lift. I'd been so close to giving up, but ...

"Liam!"

Seeing his face—even covered in blood and filth—was the most refreshing sight I'd ever laid eyes on. I rushed him, headed straight for his arms.

My entire body trembled as I was brought into the tightest most sincere embrace and I clung to him, letting him shoulder all I'd carried on my own while we were apart. Another flood of sadness overtook me and I couldn't let go. Until this very second, I didn't think I'd ever see him again.

"Tell me you're okay," he breathed, speaking the words between frantic kisses to my mouth and face.

I nodded as I kissed him back, tasting the salt of my own tears. "I am, but ... Beth. She was trying to defend me and things just—"

Liam quieted me. "She's fine," he assured me. "We passed Errol on our way here, made sure they both had seals, and redirected him to the safe zone. Beth was coming to in his arms, healing from a nasty wound from what I could see."

I breathed another deep sigh of relief but had questions. "Seals? What safe zone?"

He ignored the inquiry but removed one of two strange necklaces from around his neck to place it around mine. Next, he took my shoulders, putting distance between us before looking me over. I guessed he just needed to see for himself that I really was okay. And when he did, I was keenly aware of the moment he took notice of how my body had changed.

A large hand splayed across my stomach and there was no mistaking the look behind his eyes. No, this was not the time for emotional reunions, but relief swelled within him at the realization that we were *both* okay. Our safety, our *survival*, meant everything to him.

His gaze moved past me, over my shoulder to the remains still smoldering on the floor. I didn't have the heart to explain or even identify whose body lie there, but ... he seemed to know. I guessed as much when he didn't ask questions.

There were more footsteps and then silence. My heart sank even before I had the courage to glance up, seeing the color drain from Roz's face as she stood frozen.

"Is that ..." she mumbled, unable to finish her question, maybe for fear of what my answer might be.

I didn't have the heart to confirm, didn't have the heart to tell her the boy she loved had sacrificed himself.

She slumped against the wall and sank to the floor, staring as water filled her eyes ... as her heart broke.

I would have taken it all back if I could have.

Richie staggered in next, both his brothers right behind him. Finally, Chris and Lucas followed. The moment they laid eyes on Nick their gazes shifted to me. There was no blame or accusation, just confusion and ... overwhelming sadness.

I was certain they could tell by the blood streaked down my chest, stomach, and arms that this struggle hadn't been one-sided. Still, I had to say something.

"He ... saved me," I choked out, wanting them all to know that, despite what Nick had become, despite the hell we'd been through trying to find a way around the curse for all parties involved, his heart was still good. Pure right to the very end.

"He could have killed me after Beth escaped, but somehow, he fought it and ... he did what he could to save me." I barely got through the sentence. Their sense of loss was so powerful in the room.

A gentle kiss went to the top of my hair and my eyes closed at the feel of it. Liam, although relieved by having found me alive, seemed to be feeling something else. I couldn't quite place what it was at first, but when he addressed Richie, I identified it.

Sympathy.

For Nick, his brothers.

"I'm sorry," he shared. "It should have never come to this."

He was completely right. There should have been no need for the curse centuries ago. A curse that resulted in a loss I, nor the others, would ever get over.

"He deserves better than to be left here like this," Liam said before making an offer. "I'll help with his body."

He took a step away from me to give the others a hand.

I removed the torn cloak and laid it over Nick first. No one said a word as they came closer and lifted him from the ground, the six acting as pallbearers to a fallen soldier.

As heavy as my heart was, I knew Roz's was a million times heavier. She cared for Nick deeply. Despite his flaws, despite the changes he'd undergone recently. I believe he knew her true feelings and they were mutual.

She and I had never been close, but the experience of being a girl with a broken heart was universal. There wasn't a woman alive who hadn't felt it to some degree. I'd been there myself, when I thought I'd lost Liam. I wanted to comfort her, wanted her to know she wasn't alone, despite what she must have felt on the inside.

I extended my hand and, eventually, she took it, letting me help her from the ground where she rested.

"Let's get out of here," I said quietly as we exited together, following behind the others.

My brothers had been waiting there. I imagined they must have overheard and thought it best not to interrupt. However, when the brood laid eyes on me, they swooped in like a swarm. Their hugs, their love, was overwhelming in the best way.

I was reminded of the vision I had of them. It was the first inkling I had of our closeness from before and it left a lasting impression on me. I felt a connection to them from the first day they returned, but now it had deepened to the point of surpassing all understanding.

Each locked me in a tight embrace before the next pulled on me for their turn. But as soon as I was released, I went back to Roz. Making sure she wasn't alone after suffering such a great loss was my main priority.

"Dallas, is everyone all clear?"

I turned to Liam when he spoke through the walkie talkie.

"Affirmative. Beth and Errol just made it, and Hilda & Company took care of all the witchy business," Dallas replied.

"And the spell's holding? None of the soldiers or dragons without the seal were able to escape the area?"

"Affirmative," Dallas repeated. "The only shifters who made it out were our own."

Listening to their conversation, I realized how organized this rescue mission had been. They'd thought beyond retrieving Beth and me, but took measures to ensure that when this ended, it was really over.

For good.

"All right," Liam went on. "Sebastian and Blaise were taken care of and we're on our way out. When I give you the signal, tell Hilda and Elise to nuke this place."

When he was done speaking, he turned to make sure we were still all together. Meanwhile, my mind was stuck on one bit of information he'd conveyed to Dallas during that conversation.

Sebastian and Blaise were dead.

With that news, it felt like I could breathe for the first time since finding out the Sovereign even existed. His reign had been one of death and tyranny. He'd been the long arm of the law his people were unjustly forced to submit to, and now ... he was gone.

I'd never been happier leaving anyplace behind in my entire life. It was a day of victories and tragic loss. At the thought, I glanced toward Nick, his body covered as his brothers and friends carried him with us. This walk was a solemn one as each of us reflected on our journeys—both as individuals and together.

An unlikely alliance had been forged between us. A bond that had been tested repeatedly. And in the end, we stood as one solid unit that had proven we could stand against anything.

We reached the top of a hill and stepped over a thick ring of what looked like salt. I, for one, felt lighter immediately, like a weight had been lifted from my shoulders.

Liam's arm went around me, and the woods were eerily silent as he brought the walkie talkie to his mouth again. But this time, he only said one word.

"Now."

A strong wind rushed past us and I shivered, watching as its force caused the grass to bow beneath it, caused thick tree branches to shutter. It moved like a constant, invisible wave all the way to the center of town, and then, just as quickly as the atmosphere went still ... a brilliant turquoise flash lit up the night sky, expanding to cover all of Ridge Borough.

I leaned into Liam's side as agonizing screams rose into the air, the howls of Sebastian's lycans and dragons being consumed by the blue flame of an original—our clan's failsafe to ensure that we would never have to live through another era of hell.

I turned away from the blaze, glancing up at Liam. The sweetest part of all was that finally, for the first time in our lives, there was no threat of *anything* tearing us apart. He was mine and I was his.

Forever.

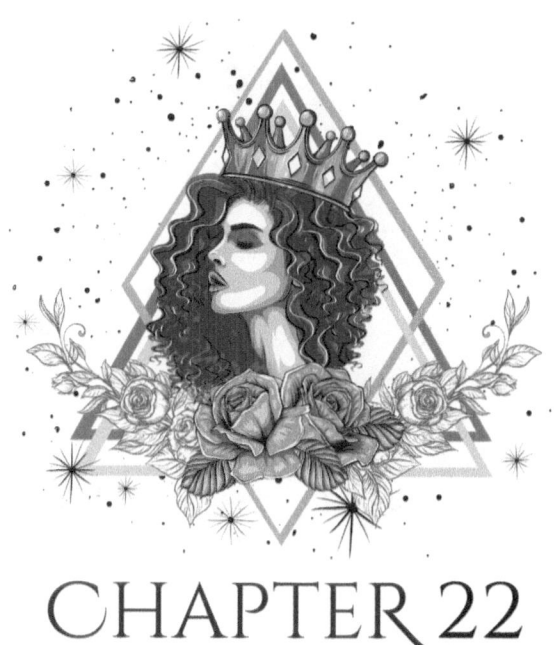

CHAPTER 22

Two Weeks Later ...

Evie

This garden was now so familiar. I'd seen it from the terrace in my dreams countless times, but this was the first time I walked through it.

My eyes stayed trained on my feet, staring as a long, blue dress trailed through the grass. At either side, stones outlined the path. It only took a moment to realize I wasn't alone, a moment to understand the sense of being surrounded by love to overwhelm me.

I glanced right and my gaze landed on a face that shouldn't have been familiar to me, but it was. At the sight of his dark skin creasing with a broad smile—the kind that made his eyes crinkle at the corners—my heart filled with emotion. To the point that I believed it might actually burst. I knew him, knew beyond the shadow of a doubt that he was Noah.

My father.

"I thought I'd join you," he said, the smoothness of his deep, soothing voice ringing familiar to my senses. "I hope you don't mind the company."

I took his hand and felt so safe, so loved. "I'm glad to have you," I replied, resting my head on his shoulder as our pace slowed.

The breeze kissed my face just like the heat of the sun high above. I recalled Liam saying once that the garden was one of my favorite places. Being here now, even in a dream, I understood why. There was so much peace. It inspired me to reflect and seek clarity.

"Your mother is concerned," he said, breaking the silence.

My smile dimmed a bit before replying. "Why would she be concerned?"

A flock flew overhead, and while I had zero knowledge of birds present day, I couldn't say the same for the old me. I was able to identify them without a second thought—white-tailed swallows.

I lowered my gaze, keeping my eyes trained on the path ahead, and listened when my father replied.

"She fears you were overwhelmed by your new charge."

My stomach sank hearing him acknowledge it, and I didn't respond.

We walked in silence for a moment before he spoke again.

"Do you know why I chose you?"

I breathed deep.

"I was a bit confused," I admitted. "I'm unsure why you'd over-look my brothers, your own sons."

A deep sigh left my mouth. Just acknowledging the task he'd given me—one day inheriting the kingdom—made me feel incredibly overwhelmed.

His eyes were so gentle when he stopped walking and turned to face me. "I can see why this would be difficult to understand."

"Most fathers cannot wait to see their eldest son follow in his footsteps. Declan is strong, noble, certainly fit to be king," I argued.

My father nodded. "I agree with everything you've said."

"Then why would you put this responsibility on me?" I snapped, immediately regretting the tone I'd taken with him. "I'm ... I apologize," I said, humbling myself.

He hadn't let the harshly spoken words rattle him. Instead, he seemed to sympathize as my hands were taken into his. The same peace that rested on him throughout our conversation took a hold of me, too, as my eyes roamed his features. He was regal, handsome.

"Evangeline, the crown will one day be yours because ... this is your calling. Appointing you was not a choice ... it was my responsibility," he declared.

I didn't understand what he could have meant by this, so I said nothing.

His hand was warm when he settled it against my cheek, smiling as he held my gaze. "One day you will understand. It may be when you're seated on the throne, overlooking your people, but ... you'll understand," he promised.

For now, I'd just have to trust his word.

I was brought into a hug and more words were whispered into my ear. "No matter what, I'll always watch over you."

My father's promise lingered in my thoughts as the dream faded and daylight seeped through the blinds in Liam's bedroom. Seemed like all I'd done the past couple weeks was sleep, but according to Elise, that was to be expected as I neared the end, as the baby grew at an even more rapid rate than before.

At the thought, my eyes drifted down to where the white sheet covered the bulge beneath it, now three times the size it was when I escaped. Inside, my son or daughter wielded a powerful kick that made me smile when I placed my hand there.

Peace ... we finally had peace.

Thankfully, Beth healed from the wounds that would have been fatal had they been sustained by a human. After a bit of medical attention from a nurse within the clan, a few days in bed was all she needed to be back on her feet. She'd been over to visit so often I worried she might slow the healing, but she wouldn't hear of it. I shouldn't have been surprised, though. She'd more than proven that the bounds of our friendship were limitless, and I would never take her loyalty for granted.

If there was one thing I took away from all this, it's that, at the end of the day, friends and family were what made the world go round. One didn't need celebrity status or millions in the bank. All I needed were a few good-hearted people who reciprocate the love you give.

That's it.

Also adding to the extreme calm I felt since making it home was that Ivan was on the mend, too. When all the witches were rounded up and seized in Ridge Borough, they managed to single out the one responsible for the spell placed on the arrow that nearly killed him. She undid her magic and was then sentenced to death, while a few of her constituents received a lesser sentence.

Upon being interrogated by Hilda and a large, neighboring coven, it was decided that not all joined Sebastian's ranks at freewill. Apparently, he'd forcefully seized a handful of young witches to do his dirty work, so instead of death, they were exiled to the Isle of Rayma. From my understanding, that was often considered a fate *worse* than death. The entire island was hidden from the outside world by magic. It was also lawless and crawling with rogue criminals of the supernatural variety. In short, all our Sebastian-related problems had been eradicated and we were all better off that way.

With both Ivan and Beth back on their feet, our clan was almost complete.

Almost.

I still felt the loss of Nick as heavily as if it had just taken place. Losing him stung in ways I couldn't even put to words. And it wasn't lost on me that he played a huge part in me being here. Had it not been for that single selfless act, my family would have laid me to rest and I would have missed out on this beautiful life I'd been given.

Not an hour passed that I didn't think of him, how he sacrificed himself so I could live, so my child could live. He'd taught me so much—about friendship, about loyalty. I'd never forget him for what he'd given me.

A chance to finally have the life I'd lost.

I glanced over at the rising sun outside my window and smiled at the beautiful gift of living to see another day.

"Thank you, Nick," I whispered, knowing I'd never take waking up in the morning for granted ever again.

A soft knock at the door stole my attention, and then the knob turned. Liam stuck his head inside to see if I was up and I smiled.

"Thought you'd still be asleep," he said, stepping in with one hand behind his back.

I tried to peek, but he hid whatever he carried well. He'd been keeping something from me. I could tell. There were whispered conversations between he and Elise, my brothers, Hilda. Several nights in a row, I'd awakened to find he'd gone missing. And now this morning, he'd been out and about already.

"Please tell me there's a bagel, donut, or *something* edible behind your back."

That beautiful smile of his flashed and he came closer, revealing a long-stemmed rose instead of food. Just as good ...

"I have a request," he said quietly, easing onto the bed to place a kiss just beneath my ear. Right after, the sheet that covered my stomach was eased down and my shirt lifted. A second kiss was placed there as he pressed a hand to my side. He couldn't get enough of feeling his son or daughter rolling around in there. Neither could I.

"What *sort* of request?" I finally replied.

"The kind that requires you to get dressed and join me downstairs."

I groaned in response, sinking beneath the blanket again. "But I'm sooooo comfortable," I whined with a laugh.

My hip was braced in his massive hand and I let him pull me closer. Being near him left me with the same feeling of love and protection from *him* that I experienced during the memory of my father in the dream. I'd had one nearly every night now and I was almost certain I had the pregnancy to thank for that.

"Don't make me beg you," Liam crooned, causing me to get swept away in his hazel stare.

"But you sound so good doing it," I laughed, bringing his face to mine so I could reach his lips.

"Don't be cute," he groaned playfully, burying his face in the side of my neck.

A laugh burst from my throat and I brought him closer, remembering something I dreamed a few nights ago.

"You know what else you sound good doing?" I asked.

He pulled away slowly, still eyeing the spot on my neck he'd just kissed. "I'm listening," was his reply, and the depth of his voice added to the point I was about to make.

"Singing."

"And that's my cue to leave," he announced, one corner of his mouth tugging up into a half smile. As soon as the words touched my ears, he moved to stand, but stopped when I caught his arm.

"Wait! I wasn't even gonna ask for a song," I laughed. "It's just something I saw and heard a few nights ago. In a memory that came to me," I clarified.

But that honestly hadn't been the only time. The first was when I wandered inside his head while he drove, unaware that I was present with him. Before getting his attention, he'd been singing one of my mother's favorite songs—*Talihina Sky*. I hadn't forgotten that, but hearing him in the dream was a pleasant surprise.

He lowered his head and I smiled a bit at what I saw.

"Oh wow! Are you turning red, Liam?" I laughed, teasing him. "Did I actually embarrass you? The warrior known around the world as Reaper?" I went on, rubbing it in even more.

"All right, enough," he laughed, pushing a hand through his dark waves. "I was a different guy back then, so I want your word that this highly classified information will never leave this room," he added.

I crossed my heart with my finger. "I promise."

I stared after that, in awe as my cheeks ached with a grin. I still found it hard to believe he was mine. And seeing him actually being shy about this was kinda sweet.

"It's been cool having you remember, though," he said, changing the conversation.

"Agreed. It still doesn't quite feel like they're my own memories yet. It's more like watching someone else's, but I don't think it will always be that way."

He kissed the back of my hand and, at the feel of it, I was overwhelmed with a sense of unmatched joy. It felt so good to be home, so good to be back with the ones I loved. Granted, there was a lot of work ahead of us as I established myself in my new position, but the Council advised me to wait until I was no longer 'in a delicate way', which suited me just fine. I'd take the time to get acclimated to motherhood, and then I'd step into my role as queen, prepared to be the leader the people had deserved for so long.

"Ten minutes," Liam said, sealing the comment with one last kiss before disappearing again.

I held the rose, sniffing it as I tried to guess what he might have needed me downstairs for. When I kept mulling over the same two or three things in my head, I decided to just get dressed and go see for myself.

I took the stairs slowly and had to laugh at how I'd begun to waddle a bit when I walked. Bracing one hand at the base of my back, I entered the living room and was surprised to see that Liam wasn't the only one who waited for me.

Hilda greeted me with a smile and came to take my hand.

"We'll be taking a little ride," she grinned. "You'll need a light jacket."

Confused, I let her lead me back to the foyer I'd just passed through where I was handed a pair of shoes.

"I don't understand. Where are we going?"

No one answered. They just got their things on and filed out the front door where they piled into two vehicles—my brothers in Liam's pickup, which would be driven by Dallas. Hilda held onto my hand as she pulled me toward Elise's car where Liam held the passenger side door open. I passed him a curious glance as he helped me down into my seat. There was definitely a grin as he closed me in.

He and Hilda climbed into the back and Elise got behind the steering wheel. Her engine started and two guards opened the large gate to let us pass through. The suspense was killing me, but then a thought occurred to me. I'd made a request the moment we made it back home. It was that a memorial be set up for Nick, something to commemorate his bravery and the major impact he had on all our lives.

He deserved that recognition and much more.

Content that I'd figured it out, I settled into my seat and decided I wouldn't ask anymore questions. Instead, I gazed out the window at our beautiful town. The scenery was familiar as we traveled further uphill, not slowing until we came to a long driveway.

The home was massive and, from what I could recall, I hadn't been here before.

I peered up at the ivy-covered brick when we stopped out front. Three of the car doors opened and Liam came to help me from my seat. His expression still gave nothing away, but I was now second-guessing my original theory about the memorial. This was kind of a strange early-morning stop, but I assumed there was a point to it.

Liam held his hand to my lower back as we ascended the stone stairs that led to a beautifully carved front door. I expected them to stop there, to ring the bell or knock, but they simply walked in.

There was no sound and I found myself wondering if someone lived here or if it was vacant. I gave Liam another bewildered glance and, this time, he smiled a bit.

"Okay, so ... is anyone gonna tell me why we're here?"

Behind me, one of my brothers snickered when I asked.

"Are we moving and someone forgot to tell me?" was my next question.

Elise stepped forward and her big smile and wide eyes made it clear she was about to burst from holding in whatever this secret was no one was sharing with me.

"We've been hiding something," she began, "but I assure you, it's not whatever you're thinking."

The statement only made me *more* confused.

"Don't be upset that we kept it secret, but ... the entire process would've been too emotional for us to involve you," Dallas explained.

"In case things didn't quite go according to plan," Elise rushed to add, nearly bouncing out of her expensive shoes with excitement as she explained.

"Any guesses?" Ivan asked.

I turned, so happy to see him on his feet again. "I ... no. I don't have a clue, but you all are making my heart race," I said with a laugh, feeling their excitement transfer to me.

I was all out of guesses, so I then decided to throw my original theory out as bait, wondering if I'd somehow been on track and just didn't realize it yet.

"The first things that came to mind was the memorial for Nick," I shared. "I thought you all might have put something together ..."

My voice trailed off when no one confirmed.

Elise's smile grew. "We ... might have done a little better than that."

She took my hand and I glanced over at Liam as I was led past the grand staircase toward a long hallway to my left. Statues lined the broad space and we passed a beautiful library. Yes, this place held someone's belongings, but still felt unoccupied.

I was so incredibly confused that I eventually stopped guessing what the surprise might be. Even as I was taken close to a set of French doors at the end of the hall. They were partially open and faint voices wafted in, but ...

"Who's out there?" I asked, turning to direct the question toward Liam.

He didn't change his stance, still opting not to answer.

I turned toward the door again as the voices came in louder and, for a moment, I ... I thought I recognized one of them, but ... what I *thought* I heard was impossible.

When my bewildered gaze shifted from Elise to Hilda, both nodded toward the doors, encouraging me to pass through them. So, I stepped closer and, when I did, had it not been for Liam moving forward to steady me on my feet, I might have gotten weak in the knees with what I saw.

With *who* I saw.

There, seated in a chair with his back to me ... a headful of brown hair. And that voice as he sat across from friends—Chris, Lucas, Beth, and a very happy, smiling Roz. It sounded just like ...

" ... Nick."

His name tumbled from my lips in a whisper because I only half-believed my eyes. With the vivid dreams I had lately, I didn't quite trust what I was seeing. He shouldn't have been here. Shouldn't have been sitting on this patio, breathing.

I was stunned when I was no longer staring at the back of a head, but into a set of blue eyes that had brought me so much comfort. Tears welled, clouding my vision.

"How are—"

He stood, his foreboding stature blocking out the sun from behind as he came closer, causing my head to tilt back as I stared up in disbelief.

Those tears that welled flowed freely now as emotion overwhelmed me. I'd seen him pass away with my own two eyes, had held his hand as he transitioned. So how was he ... *here?*

A broad hand stretched toward me, and despite not knowing whether I was awake or still dreaming, I took it, feeling the warmth of his palm against mine.

He chuckled a bit, taking in my wide eyes and gaping mouth.

"It's really me, Evie," he stated, only making me question things more instead of assuring me I was really seeing this, really *living* this.

Liam's hand braced my shoulder before he spoke. "We couldn't tell you because, well, being honest, there was no guarantee it would even work. There were so many unknowns that came into play, we ..."

I glanced up at him, cutting him off. "He's ... this is real?" I asked, feeling my lips quiver with the question.

Liam's smile broadened, seeing my excitement. When he nodded, it only brought on more tears. "It's real."

I turned, laying eyes on Nick again, and I could only think of one thing to do.

I threw my arms around his neck.

Things felt so different. After the darkness that hung over us fell away as I sat beside his body on the floor of the church weeks ago, I felt so much lighter. And now, as we embraced, it was so good to hold him and not hear that nagging voice in the back of my mind telling me he was dangerous, telling me that, despite the love I had for him, I ought to keep my distance. No, as we hugged now, I felt none of those negative things. Only peace.

"How is this even possible?" I asked, not really needing the details. All that mattered was that he was here.

"Well, we have Liam and Elise to thank," Nick shared. "They took a huge chance on me, and ... I can't even begin to say how grateful I am."

It was so strange to hear him speak of Liam in a positive light, so strange to hear that *he* had played a part in Nick being here.

"I still don't get it," I said, laughing amidst happy tears. "But I'm too excited to care."

He laughed, too, and the sound of it was like music to my ears. I didn't think I'd ever hear it again.

When he leaned away I peered up, unsure of what he'd say next.

"I want to explain it, but maybe I can show you better than I can tell you," he stated, piquing my interest with the obscure statement, but then ... it wasn't so obscure anymore.

He held out his palm and, half a second later my breath ceased.

There was a flame.

My heart skipped a beat at the sight of it, feeling the pieces begin to fall into place.

"It was Elise," Liam spoke up from behind me.

Bewildered, I kept my eyes trained on Nick's hand, trying to wrap my mind around the idea of him being a ... *dragon*.

"You never told me how cool this was," he chuckled, closing his hand and extinguishing the light inside it. "Flying is like ... it's the best part."

I turned to Liam, playfully scowling at him. "Flying?" I asked. "You made me wait like six months to learn!"

He chuckled as I glared at him. "Kid's been through lot," Liam commented. "Figured he earned it."

The two exchanged a look and, for the first time ever, I sensed an air of respect between them—the love of my life and one of the best friends a girl could ever ask for. Seeing them in one another's presence without one wanting to tear the other limb from limb was like a dream come true.

"Is this where you've been coming when you disappear?" I asked, already knowing what Liam's answer would be.

He nodded, confirming that Nick had been the one stealing his time from me. The middle-of-the-night runs, waking up in bed alone morning after morning. But now, as I gazed up at the newest dragon in Seaton Falls, the lost time was definitely worth it.

I hugged Nick again, couldn't help it.

Over his shoulder, Roz stood with a content smile you could have seen from the moon. She had her love back—a feeling I could certainly relate to.

I released Nick and let myself take it all in. At first, I believed I'd have to accept not having total happiness. While family meant everything to me ... friendship was incredibly high on that list, too.

And now, I really and truly had it all.

"Thank you," I said, peering up at Nick, stating the same words I said to myself since returning home. Only, this time, I finally got to say it to his face. "I owe you my life."

He responded with a brilliant smile and an offer.

"Well, once you're able," he said, glancing down at my

stomach with only joy in his expression, "I think I know how you can repay me."

I chuckled a bit. "Oh, yeah? How?"

He took a deep breath and turned to look out on the property of what I now guessed to be his grandfather's estate.

"I've got a lot to learn about being a dragon," he began. "I was wondering if there might be a queen with a little spare time to show me the ropes."

My cheeks hurt with how hard I smiled at that. "Well, it just so happens I know a queen with her whole life ahead of her."

His lips curved up with a nostalgic grin. "It's a date?"

I reached for Liam, clutching his hand in my left as I felt beyond blessed to have it all. When I reached for Nick's with my right, I confirmed with a promise.

"It's a date."

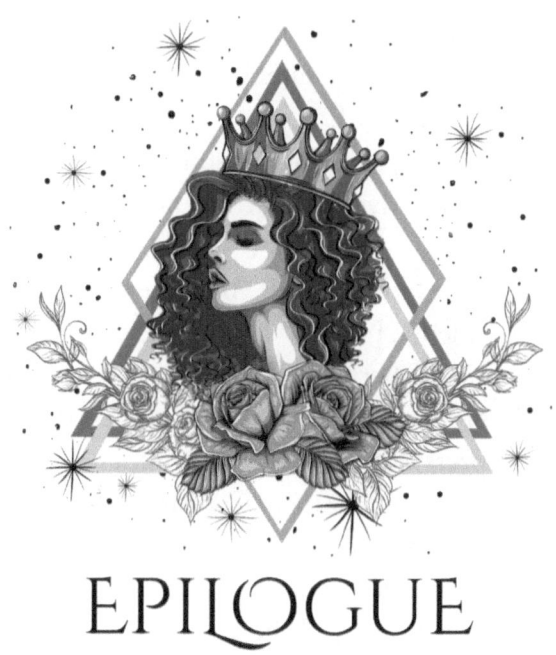

EPILOGUE

Two Weeks Later ...

Liam

I hadn't taken my eyes off her since she came into the world three hours ago. I'd never seen anything more perfect in my entire life.

Figures, seeing as how she was the spitting image of her mother. From the dark curls framing her small face, to the flecks of green in her eyes like mine, she was one-hundred-percent us.

One-hundred-percent made from love.

Before this, it was hard to imagine myself as a father, but now that she had arrived, it felt like I finally found my purpose. A small yawn and tiny stretch brought a smile out of me like I'd just won the lottery. I suppose, in many ways, I had.

My gaze drifted to Evangeline where she lay sleeping. I marveled at the strength she showed today. I was by her side the entire time and there wasn't anything in this world that could have pulled me away. I witnessed a miracle today.

The birth of our little girl.

With things being upside down before, there hadn't been time to think of a name in advance, but the moment Evangeline laid eyes on her she knew.

In honor of her father Noah, the latest descendent of his legacy would be called ... Noelle.

The sliver of space between the door and the frame widened as Hilda poked her head inside. Her gaze landed right on her new niece and her expression warmed. She stepped inside, quietly to avoid waking Evangeline. I stood from my seat beside the bed, already knowing why she'd come.

My arms immediately felt the loss when I handed Noelle over. I wanted to keep her there until she, *herself,* was old enough to tell me I had to let go. I'd been a protector for so long, and now I knew that feeling would only deepen as I watched her grow.

"You're absolutely beautiful, little one," Hilda whispered, running a hand down Noelle's head. The motion smoothed her thick curls. "It was an honor to help bring you into the world," she added, placing a kiss on her forehead.

Hilda had been at Evangeline's side the whole time. She was skilled with this sort of thing—having helped deliver countless children within the kingdom in centuries past. It was that expertise that kept Evangeline comfortable and kept me from worrying myself to death. In the end, everything worked out exactly as it was supposed to.

Elise stayed close, too, insistent on witnessing the moment her first grandchild came into existence. And the second she did, there were so many tears.

In the recent past, none of us were certain we'd get here—to peace, to happiness—so to now have it all was a gift.

The most priceless gift I'd ever received.

Hilda's gaze shifted to Evangeline as she swayed, keeping Noelle content. "Has Mom asked for anything?"

I smiled hearing her refer to Evangeline that way. "She's been out for a couple hours now. I imagine she'll be starving when she wakes up, though."

"Then I'll prepare a meal," Hilda offered. "Something grand, considering the occasion."

She was right; this *was* a special occasion. The most important of my life, actually.

Hilda fell silent and I took note of the thoughtful look she wore.

"Something wrong?"

She peered up. "Wrong? No."

"But ..."

She smiled when I didn't let her off the hook so easily. "It's just that ... I sense something."

"With Noelle?" I asked, hearing the concern in my own tone.

"Settle down," Hilda laughed. "Everything's fine. It's just that ... I believe she's special. More special than any of us could have foreseen."

I had no clue what that meant, but judging by the jovial expression she wore, I now knew whatever she spoke of was nothing to worry about.

I took a seat on the edge of the bed when she dropped down into my chair. "Our princess has a unique energy," she began. "Almost as if she possesses some sort of ... magic."

My brow quirked. "Magic? As in ... the kind witches possess?"

She nodded. "It's entirely possible and I'm rarely wrong about these things. If you'll recall, I had it right when I said Evangeline didn't have an ounce of it in her, despite Elise insisting otherwise," she laughed.

I smiled a bit, but still didn't understand.

"She was conceived while you were human, therefore, she's

half human, which would make it more likely for the abilities of *my* lineage to break through."

I remembered something Hilda said before, something the Oracles alluded to. It was in regards to our daughter being *'highly sought after'* because she'd be different. Hearing Hilda's theory now only made me more grateful we were able to cancel Sebastian's plans before her arrival. With him gone, any and all threats to her life had been eliminated.

Even the one Nick posed.

I stared at Noelle in Hilda's arms and couldn't imagine her not being here. I would've missed out on everything had it gone differently that night. It wasn't lost on me that we were a mere breath away from all our lives being completely unrecognizable. Had Nick not been able to resist the curse, I would have lost my family. Had Evangeline's dragon not showed herself, causing Nick's life to be taken by fire, we wouldn't have been able to bring him back. At the thought of it, the way Nick had sacrificed himself, I knew I would forever be indebted to him.

He hadn't only given *Evangeline* a second chance.

He'd given *me* one as well.

So many had stopped by in the last two weeks—friends who wanted to check in, wanted to ask if we needed anything, but none had been here as often as Nick. I could only imagine what it must feel like to have the burden of his curse finally off his back, to know he was free to live his life without worrying he'd one day become something he'd hate.

It didn't take him long to get comfortable in his new shifted form. Mostly, he liked that becoming his dragon was far less painful than turning into a wolf had been. His brothers were only grateful we found a way to bring him back, even if it did change him. As Richie put it, he was still their brother, still a member of the pack.

There were so many moving pieces, so many unknown factors

that had come into play … one might think we had someone looking out for us.

Like Noah.

The more I thought about it, I believed Hilda's theory was dead on as usual. Noah had always been a protector when he was living, it wasn't so far fetched to think he would be one in the afterlife as well, looking after his only daughter like he promised.

"I suppose I should go get started on this meal," Hilda said with a groan as she stood. Noelle was in my arms the next second and I wasn't ashamed to admit I missed having her there.

It was just the three of us again and I turned toward Evangeline when she squirmed. A few seconds later, big, brown eyes were fixed on me, and there was so much love behind them, I felt it.

"You're still here," she said with a raspy whisper, smiling when her gaze locked with mine, and then slipped to Noelle.

"Where else would I go?" I asked. "Everything I'll ever need is right here in this room."

Her smile grew and the feeling of contentment that hadn't left me in weeks did the same.

"Did she give you any trouble while I was out?" she asked.

I glanced down at the beauty I held. "Not even a little."

"That's because, hands down, in your arms is *the* best place to be on Earth," she teased with a yawn. "Seriously. I can't even blame the girl. She learns fast."

I laughed. Between the two of us, I was definitely the lucky one.

I eased back against the headboard. Evangeline automatically leaned in and my arm went around her. I now had *both* my girls close.

She placed her hand on top of the tiny one against my chest.

"We really do have it all, don't we?" she asked.

"More than I ever imagined." And that was the honest truth.

For the first time ever, I felt whole and it was all because of her. And judging by the smile that hadn't left her face in weeks, I was pretty sure she felt the same.

So many things we lost had been given back to us, restored in ways we never thought possible. Even Evangeline's love for Rebecka and Todd hadn't come back void. With a little encouragement, she put in a call to her parents a few nights ago. It turned out that the number her mother had given the night of the flood was still good. Grateful for the sacrifice Evangeline made for them, they insisted she come visit in Chicago soon. No, their memory of her would never return, but I had a feeling their love for her hadn't faded. They might not understand why the girl they believed to be a stranger had a hold on their hearts, but they seemed open to keeping in touch. I loved the hope and peace this brought Evangeline. It was more than she ever thought she'd have.

"You've given me everything a man could ever want," I admitted, placing a kiss in her hair the next second.

She looked up with a smile and I knew there was nothing to bring me down from this high.

'And you're the best warrior a girl could ever ask for,' she said back, her thoughts bleeding into mine.

Our love was so strong it caused our worlds to collide twice. Some might consider that fate, nature's way of bringing things full circle. In the coming months, as she stepped into her destiny, those of us who loved her would be there every step of the way. And as long as we were, she'd have the chance to reign in peace.

With Evangeline finally seated in her rightful place, our realm had hope, something we hadn't been afforded in so long. Through her, the legacy of history's most powerful kingdom had finally been restored, and there was no doubt in my mind or heart she'd wear the crown with honor.

With nobility.

Forever.

Long live the queen.

Need more dragons?
Since you've just finished reading Noelle's origin story, take a peek
into the future while hanging out with some of your favorite
Seaton Falls shifters in an adventurous spinoff!
The Dragon Fire Academy series takes love, bravery, and loyalty to
a whole new level. Follow Noelle—Evie and Liam's greatest legacy
—as she embarks on a journey of her own.

This is a complete upper YA/NA series that features a reverse
harem romance. Noelle is on the cusp of her twentieth birthday
and her initial shift. Come find out what happens when she heads
off to a beautiful island academy where four dragon guardians first
test her patience, and then her heart.
Find the cover and synopsis below!

Love ARCs, random giveaways, and fun bookish conversation?
Come hang out in my Facebook group for readers,
THE SHIFTER LOUNGE!
https://www.facebook.com/groups/141633853243521
Can't wait to chat with you :)
For all feedback and inquiries, email me at author.racheljonas@
gmail.com

THE LOST ROYALS SAGA

A NOTE FROM THE AUTHOR

Thank you so much for reading Fate of the Fallen, *The Lost Royals Saga, Book 5.*

If you have enjoyed entering the world of the Lost Royals, show other readers by leaving a review!
Just visit my website for all available portals where to review the book:
https://www.racheljonasauthor.com

Join my readers' group for more news The Shifter Lounge
https://www.facebook.com/groups/141633853243521
and my Newsletter today!
https://us14.list-manage.com/subscribe?u=
73f44054c9dda516cc713aea7&id=ad3ee37cf1

THE LOST ROYALS SAGA

NEXT FROM RACHEL JONAS

There's a spinoff of the Lost Royals Saga!
Own the DRAGON FIRE ACADEMY trilogy today!

Four dragon warriors.
A beautiful shifter hybrid.
An island with a dark secret that could bring them all to their knees.

Seriously? Four dragon warriors need to stalk my every move? I get it; they think I'm dangerous, but I'm only on their island to learn. Not to destroy it.

This is another unfortunate side-effect of being the freak who descended from all three supernatural lineages. The bloodthirsty dragons, the destructive wolves, and the disloyal witches. Some believe that, when I transition in a few months, there's a slight, teeny tiny chance I could unleash hell on the supernatural world. Call me crazy, but I'd know if I harbored that kind of power inside me.

... Wouldn't I?

My entire life, all I've wanted was to be normal. Hence the reason I didn't think twice about trading in my crown for a stack of books. I've got three terms on this island to prove the naysayers wrong, including my chaperones—Kai, Ori, Paulo, and Rayen.

These four are gorgeous, but also ominous as heck. Babysitting me has clearly taken their focus off something they've deemed more important. So, now they go out of their way to make my life a living hell, with hopes that I'll give up and leave.

Thanks, guys.

You could cut the tension between us with a knife, but what's weird is I don't hate them all the time. There are even odd moments when I catch them watching me. And not in their usual "wish-you-were-dead" sort of way.

Even if I survive the academy, there's still no guarantee these four and I won't kill each other before graduation.

Grab book 1 now!
https://www.racheljonasauthor.com

THE LOST ROYALS SAGA

ABOUT THE AUTHOR

Rachel Jonas also writes as Nikki Thorne.

Hey, I'm Rachel! Consider this your formal invitation to hang out in my private Facebook group, THE SHIFTER LOUNGE. You'll get fun book convo, exclusive giveaways, and other random acts of nerdiness!

Don't usually talk to strangers? No worries! Allow me to introduce myself. I'm a Michigan native, wife, and mother of three who made a career of indulging the voices inside my head :) With several completed series, and stories in both the paranormal and contemporary YA/NA romance categories, there's something for everyone!

Happy reading!

Don't forget to follow me!

Twitter: @author_R_Jonas
IG: @author.racheljonas
Rachel's Facebook: https://www.facebook.com/author
racheljonas/
Reader Group:
https://www.facebook.com/groups/141633853243521/
Amazon: amzn.to/2BHiLlS
Goodreads:
https://www.goodreads.com/author/show/16788419.
Rachel_Jonas
BookBub: https://www.bookbub.com/profile/rachel-jonas
Nikki's Facebook: https://www.facebook.com/nikkithorneauthor/
TikTok: https://www.tiktok.com/@racheljonasauthor